THREE KINGS

Freydís Moon

ISBN: 9798853979840

Cover Illustration and Interior Artwork by M.E. Morgan

Praise For ☽

Olivia Waite named *Heart, Haunt, Havoc* a New York Times Best Romance Book of 2023

"Told in beautiful prose and stunning style, *Three Kings* is the perfect read to cozy up on a cold, chilly day. It was heartwarming, thoughtful, and sincerely honest in its brilliant handling of topics such as pregnancy, family-building, and the magic that binds us all."

—**DC Guevara** author of *A Vermilion Curse*

"Eerie as a haunting, biting as the midwinter night, and as tender as the ache of new love, *Heart, Haunt, Havoc* lingers long past the last page."

—**K. M. Enright** author of *Mistress of Lies*

"[*Three Kings is*] full of healing, intimacy, and interpersonal devotion, this autumnal read is perfect for people looking for some magic and tenderness a la a Miyazaki film..."

　—**Ladz** author of *Ice Upon a Pier*

"*With A Vengeance* is a dark, visceral exploration of queerness, eroticism, trauma, racism, and recovery that sinks its teeth in early and doesn't let go even after the last page. The way Moon handles 'taboo' topics and all their thorny parts is realistic, relatable, and tackled brilliantly through a main character who is neither perfect nor irredeemable... A truly stunning and poignant work of dark erotica from an author you won't forget anytime soon."

　—**Kellen Graves** author of *Prince of the Sorrows*

"As a devotee of Southwest Gothic who is acutely aware of the role of the church in our everyday lives growing up queer in New Mexico, I proudly hail [*Exodus 20:3*] as one of the most authentic and immersive examples of the genre... This tale means so much to me. I felt seen and heard and understood, but above all, I felt welcome."

　—**R.M. Virtues** author of *Sing Me to Sleep*

"Freydís has created something truly exquisite... Their writing is lush, building the atmosphere into something both familiar and magical. Reading *Exodus 20:3* feels like a religious experience, leaving you in awe by the end, wishing for more but also entirely satisfied."

　—**Harley Laroux** author of *The Dare*

AND WHEN I WAS SHIPWRECKED
CAN'T THINK OF ALL THE COST
I THOUGHT OF YOU
ALL THE THINGS THAT WILL BE LOST NOW
IN THE CRACKS OF LIGHT
CAN WE JUST GET A PAUSE?
I DREAMED OF YOU
TO BE CERTAIN WE'LL BE TALL AGAIN
IF YOU THINK OF ALL THE COSTS
IT WAS REAL ENOUGH
WHETHER WEATHER BE THE FROST
TO GET ME THROUGH
OR THE VIOLENCE OF THE DOG DAYS
OUT ON WAVES BEING TOSSED
BUT I SWEAR
IS THERE A LINE THAT WE COULD JUST GO CROSS?
YOU WERE THERE

AND I WAS CATCHING MY BREATH
FLOORS OF A CABIN CREAKING UNDER MY STEP
AND I COULDN'T BE SURE
I HAD A FEELING SO PECULIAR
THIS PAIN WOULDN'T BE FOR
EVERMORE

TAYLOR SWIFT

CHAPTER ONE

Ethan Shaw carried two knives, one for lilies, the other for veins. The blade in his left hand curved like a smile, clipping stems at a sweet, diagonal angle. The second weapon was concealed in a petite leather sheath, tucked neatly in his right palm.

The ritual called for innocence, and he had none to spare, so he searched the shoreline for white-petaled flowers—speckled with saltwater, yawning toward the sky—and remembered the folktale that wormed through Casper, spoken quietly at the pub, hollered by sailors on the docks, cooed in the apothecary, and sung by children on the playground.

Those Casper lilies, the story went, *are filled to the brim with what we've lost.*

Like snakes, the townsfolk shed their innocence, leaving it to stew in the bay, sink into the soil, and beat against the lighthouse. And like snakes, the lilies drew their outgrown magic into tangled roots and narrow stems and gilded pollen: an ouroboros consuming itself.

Most people refused to use the term—*magic*—but Ethan found it appropriate. Harvesting long-gone energy from a living thing felt like its very definition. Using said magic to reanimate a corpse felt less like magic, though, and more like recklessness.

After another unsteady step, he lost his footing, swatting helplessly at the air. He yelped and flailed before he hit the water, bracing for the icy shock. Panic shot through him. Salt water rushed into his nostrils, and seaweed snagged his ankle. *Swim, idiot.* November wind nipped his face when he breached, sucking at the air, clutching drenched flowers to his chest. Casper lilies never promised to be easy, of course. But Ethan Shaw still cursed as he slushed through tidepools and mud. He sighed, relieved, when his soggy shoes hit the gravel path outside the tower.

"We need a lightkeeper, Ethan," he mocked, shouldering through the wooden door. He left his boots in a puddle on the cheeky welcome mat: *You Better Be Beer!* "It's a solid wage, Ethan. Not like it's a—" The first knife clattered on the rectangular table, then the second. Sopping flowers landed with a *splat* next to an unopened power bill. "—hard gig, Ethan. *Just take it.*" He whined through the last three words, mimicking his mother, and trudged into the washroom.

He hadn't the time for a bath, so he peeled the wet shirt from his back, unzipped his jeans, and wrestled out of his drenched binder. The chilly water had reddened his beige skin and left his boyish face chapped and raw. Droplets clung to his chestnut hair, shorn behind his ears and around the back of his skull, and worn long at his crown, hanging in messy strings over his brow. He slicked his hair back with an annoyed swipe and scrubbed lingering sea grime away with a warm cloth. He dried with a towel that smelled like gardenia and tobacco, like Peter, and set his palms on the vanity, studying his reflection.

Rabbit-framed, small-chested, wide-hipped, and delicately masculine, Ethan Shaw wasn't the optimal lightkeeper type, per se. He hadn't a beard, only annoying stubble, and carried himself on dainty, soft-pawed feet. Much as the townsfolk whispered about lilies, they whispered about him too.

Witch—hissed like a match strike in the nave and murmured by joggers at the park—wasn't entirely *un*true, but Ethan still preferred friendlier terminology. Alchemist, maybe. Magician, even.

"Take the job, Ethan," he mumbled and huffed at the mirror. "Surely the lifestyle suits you."

A job doing, literally, *anything* else would've suited him better.

The front door heaved open, and the clip-clopping of heavy boots filled the living quarters. "Why is the floor wet?" Peter mumbled. He repeated the question, hollering through the lighthouse, "Darling, why is the floor wet?"

Ethan rolled his eyes. "I slipped," he called, toeing the washroom door ajar.

Peter rounded the doorframe, square glasses crooked on his nose. Surprise shot to his face, but the expression faded, chased away by a frown.

"You didn't," he warned, snaring Ethan's reflection in a hard glare. "Ethan, we talked about this—"

"I don't need your permission," he snapped and slipped past Peter, striding confidently into the adjacent bedroom. He opened a drawer and fingered through his clothes, settling on a red sweater and corduroy trousers. "I've got the flowers; I know the ritual. Either have faith in me, or say *I told you so* if it doesn't work, but hovering like a—" He batted at Peter's broad chest. "—damn *moth* won't change my mind. How was work?"

"Long," Peter bit out. "Choppy water makes for terrible fishing, as you know. Even the local wildlife can't handle the riptide—as you know—and consistently get thrown ashore, *as you know*, and—"

"*You* brought it home, not me."

"I brought it home while it was still breathing," Peter said, exasperated. He trailed Ethan into the closet, craning over him while he searched for wool socks—matching, preferably—and then into the kitchen, sighing dramatically at the waterlogged lilies. "Where'd you put the poor thing, anyway? Is it still in the garden shed?"

"No, I tossed it in the bathtub." Ethan shot him an impatient glare. "Yes, of course, it's in the garden shed, Peter. You think I'd let a selkie loose in our home? Give me *some* credit."

"Okay, wait, hold on—*wait*." Peter feebly attempted to catch him while he bounced around the kitchen.

Ethan yanked a bowl out of the cabinet, slid both knives behind his leather belt, unfastened the lavender from a rope above the sink, and stuffed his mortar and pestle underneath his arm. Before he could make for the door, two palms clasped his waist, turning him. His beautiful, ridiculous husband wrinkled his nose. Sea-bitten copper cheeks, angular bones pressing hard against his skin. As always, Peter Vásquez looked dashing, exhausted, and worried.

"Ay Dios mío, just wait, okay?" Peter asked.

Ethan arched an eyebrow. After a strangled pause, he lifted onto his tiptoes. "*You* brought it home," he whispered and pecked Peter on the lips.

"It's a leopard seal, Ethan. Not a selkie," he said patiently, as he would to a toddler. "And it's dead because animals that get caught in bad weather sometimes *die*."

Ethan patted his cheek. "Sure, yeah. So, the next time you're caught in bad weather and someone plops you on my doorstep, I'll cash in your life insurance and call it a day. How's that sound?"

Peter winced. "You're impossible."

"And you're in my way." Perhaps that was a little too far, considering. But *impossible?* Ethan scoffed. He wasn't the one who'd mistaken a fae-beast—an extraordinarily *obvious* fae-beast, by the way—for a run-of-the-mill seal, and he wasn't the one who'd whimpered when said not-seal had stopped breathing, and he certainly wasn't the one who'd dragged a goddamn selkie home from work.

He narrowed his eyes, stepping around Peter's broad frame. "Stay here if you want, but if I don't give it the option to remove its pelt before morning, it'll stay dead. Right now, I have the chance to bring it back, whoever it is, and I'd rather not deal with a rotting corpse if I can help it. So—" He tucked the herb bundle and his tools inside the mixing bowl and carefully lifted his leather-bound grimoire from the book-stand on the countertop. "—stay or come. Your choice."

Peter fiddled with the frayed bottom of his scarf. A slouchy beanie covered his buzz cut, and a short, neatly kept beard framed his pursed lips. Dark-eyed, dark-haired, and irritatingly tall, he radiated warmth. Even then, as he gave his best attempt at sharpening, Peter granted Ethan a condescending once-over, and his stony face softened.

"What if it bites you?" he muttered, and straightened his glasses with a bent knuckle.

"My mother's exact words after I told her we were engaged," Ethan teased. He stepped into a pair of Birkenstocks, straps loose and floppy atop his feet, and shuffled through the front door. "C'mon, then. Let's go."

Reluctantly, Peter followed, catching the door with his boot before it swung into Ethan's shoulder. "*Impossible.*"

Ethan shot him a narrow-eyed glance.

As it turned out, marriage wasn't exactly what everyone made it out to be. It was coexisting in the same place, building bridges when arguments landed like grenades, worrying ceaselessly about each other, being irrevocably consumed by each other. Marriage in the fiscal sense? Simple. Money could be made and tracked and divided. Marriage in the lifetime sense? Complicated. Because love was indomitable, but it could be lost and ruined and squandered.

"Give me that," Peter grumbled. He plucked the unsteady grimoire from the crook of Ethan's elbow, allowing the bowl to sit more comfortably in his arms.

Ethan huffed. "Thank you."

Marriage was intrusive and messy, but somehow, Peter Vásquez made it easy.

The garden shed hugged the backside of the lighthouse, a small, lonesome thing overgrown with white sage. Ethan stepped over a wandering pumpkin vine and scanned the planter boxes, brimming with turnips, radishes, bushy spinach, and sweet onion, and swallowed around the tightness in his throat. Like the town gossiped about lilies and witches, it also cautioned against magic. Reckless magic, at least. A self-stirring coffee spoon or a vegetable overgrown from a gardening spell didn't ruffle many feathers. That kind of magic—parlor-trick shit—didn't cost the practitioner anything more than a headache and numb gums. But reanimation rituals, bartering spells, and harnessing power from beyond the elemental plane came with bloody price tags, and most people associated witches who practiced *that* kind of magic with danger. Seeing as Ethan could hardly reach the top shelf in the cupboard, dangerous seemed absurd. He preferred *equipped*. Knowledgeable, even. Brave or daring or—

"Careful with your wrist, all right? I'd hate to see you scar." Peter whimpered like a hound.

Ethan inhaled sharply. He did, truly, love his overbearing husband more than he cared to admit. "It's only a few drops. Won't leave a mark, I'm sure."

Warped wood panels bowed inward, and the metal roof had rusted over, twisting the unassuming garden shed into something spooky and decrepit. Around them, the ocean swayed and crashed, spraying foam across black rocks, muffling the *click* of a lock sliding free.

"Let me go first," Peter said.

"Oh, stop. It's *fine*." Ethan squeezed past him and swiped at the air, searching for the lamp string. Rope smacked his palm. He tugged, bathing the small space in artificial light.

Gardening gloves, terracotta pots, propagation jars, and bundled herbs littered the narrow table against the far wall, and various tools—rakes, shears, shovels, hoes—were propped in corners. Bulging bags of organic soil and a bucket filled with assorted seed packets littered the space. A ratty blanket carried back from *The Oyster*, Peter's fishing rig, spanned the center of the room, and an unnaturally still selkie rested atop it.

"Oh, look," Peter grumbled. "A dead seal."

"If it was dead, we'd smell it."

"Or the saltwater delayed rigor mortis—Ethan, *please*—"

"Stay or go, but if you keep whining, I will scream. I swear to God, Peter, they'll hear it on Berkshire Street. I'm not even—"

"All right, okay—fuck, just..." He tiptoed around the spotted body on the floor and dropped the grimoire on the table. "Get on with it, then."

Get on with it. Ethan snorted, mirroring Peter's path. At the table, he emptied the bowl and unsheathed the curved knife. The lilies came apart easily, peeled back like delicate skin where the stem thinned at each flower's blooming head. Pollen dusted his finger-tips—orange and mauve and stormy silver. Once the Casper lilies were disassembled and placed inside the mortar, he brushed dried lavender atop them, scenting the air like fresh laundry. Next, he dug the pestle into the floral concoction. Crushed and ground and kneaded until the lilies and lavender formed a perfumy paste. He flipped open his grimoire with two fingers.

"Have you ever done something like this?" Peter asked, peering over his shoulder.

"Not quite, no. I managed to restart your heart after Katia though. Same concept, different body." He kept his attention fixed to his old spell book and ignored the fearful twinge that followed her name. *Hurricane Katia.* The storm that'd torn Peter's boat to pieces, cut his crew from ten to six, and swallowed him whole. Ethan remembered how the pocketknife had slipped across his arm, how his blood had darkened Peter's mouth, how the sea had jolted from between his husband's blue lips. He'd begged the water to go and traded a bit of himself to evacuate it. Three years ago, kneeling on the docks while hail pelted Casper, Ethan Shaw had deemed himself miraculous and deadly.

Townsfolk called him *witch*, as they always had, but after that, they called him *necromancer* too.

Peter gripped Ethan's hip bone and leaned closer, resting his chin on the slope of his shoulder. "I'd only been out a few hours..." His breath coasted Ethan's throat. "But I hear you."

Out. Ethan wouldn't bother correcting him—he never did. *Dead* was the right word though. Deceased, gone, passed. He flipped to a sallow page titled Resurgence and dragged his index finger along the scribbled spell:

1. *Innocence harvested by or from the practitioner—sacrificial, floral, bodily, or spiritually*

2. *Connective tissue—flesh: earthen or feather*

3. *Binding blood—practitioner offering*

To bring back a living being, human or not, a witch needed to bind the spell with blood—their own or someone else's. To bring back a fae-beast who had died in a singular form but could potentially be clinging to life in another? That required the practitioner's blood, exclusively. Potency that couldn't be replicated and rarity that couldn't be found elsewhere. Despite having confidence in his blood, Ethan had never attempted to fashion a spell with Casper lilies, and he hoped the gossip was as true as it was prevalent.

"Easy enough," Ethan mumbled. He turned, bumping his up-turned nose against Peter's forehead. "Sorry, dear, but you need to move."

Peter flapped his lips, annoyed, and stepped away. He gave the selkie a wide berth and went to stand at the far corner of the shed. Arms folded, mouth tensed into a frown, watchful gaze burning holes into Ethan's back.

"Careful," Peter said again, as he tended to do.

Ethan struck a match. The flame glowed, bending away from a blackened wick as he lit a half-gone pillar candle. He shifted the crackling match to another, then a third. The shed glowed.

Air thickened, turning inward, seeking whatever strange, ethereal force stirred in Ethan's veins.

Like this, the selkie appeared pitifully animal—snout long and spotted, eyes closed, flippers tucked beneath itself. But Ethan knew fae magic. Saw the seam where its pelt lifted away, making room for the promise of longer bones, extra ribs, larger lungs. Noticed the bend in its webbed hands where knuckles pressed firmly against the backside of its second-self.

Ethan whispered to the candle, coaxing smoke to sway and billow, and guided gray plumes into the mortar. The stone bowl balanced in his palm; he gripped the needle-pointed knife in his free hand. Magic was topsy-turvy—palatable and friendly in one breath, urchin-shaped and aggressive in the next. He remembered how it'd crowded his throat, how he'd been willing to scrape away every ounce of himself if it meant getting Peter back. That was the strangest thing, he thought, how magic waited, considered, and chose. Hurricane Katia had forced Ethan to claw at the power he carried and sacrifice it unchallenged. That specific, heartsick panic didn't influence the spell with this selkie, though, and he had to prepare for what that meant.

That the ritual might not work.

That magic might not listen.

"Don't be stubborn," he whispered and knelt in front of the selkie. Its face was placid, chin resting on the floor, fur sleek and dark from brow to tail.

Peter made a childish, uncertain noise. "*Careful.*"

"I'm all right." Ethan set the bowl down and eased the tip of the blade above his palm. When the knife bit, his skin parted, allowing a red stream to snake over his heartline. The sharp pain dulled into an ache almost immediately, but he still counted his heartbeats, following the quick pulse drumming in his wound.

"Rise," he said under his breath and scooped the lily-lavender mixture onto his fingers. He pulled open the selkie's jaws, flinching at the prick of sharp teeth, and smeared the salve onto the roof of its mouth.

Magic pulsed, alive and curious, thrumming in his gums, jolting into his elbows, causing his stomach to churn. He hadn't realized he'd closed his eyes. Didn't register Peter's soft gasp or the lamp dimming or the candle flickering. Ethan felt the spell snap away and leave him, as if it'd lived in his chest, rooted there like a weed. The sensation knocked the wind from him. He almost gagged. Almost toppled over. But he cracked his eyes open instead and found the selkie staring back at him.

The leopard seal, actually. Black-eyed, sharp-toothed, inhaling and exhaling.

"Ethan..." Peter eased toward him, one shaky arm outstretched. "Maybe we should—"

The selkie lunged, snapping at Ethan's bloody hand. It barked and trilled. Whipped its head back and forth, smacked its muscular tail against the ground, and bared its teeth. Ethan fell onto his rear and scrambled backward. He hardly avoided another snap, yelping as the selkie's mouth *clicked* in front of his nose.

Before he knew it, Peter hollered, "*Jesus Christ,*" then gripped Ethan around his middle, hauling him backward.

Peter stumbled and tripped over his own feet. He fell onto the cobblestone path outside the shed, still wrapped around Ethan. The selkie barreled after them. Peter gave a girlish shout and kicked the garden shed door shut, trapping the fae-beast inside.

Ethan snarled at the creaky door. "I just saved your fucking life!"

Thankless little monster. He lurched forward, but Peter held him at bay.

"Surprise, it's a mean-ass seal," Peter said. He heaved an aggravated sigh. "Who almost *bit* you, like I said it would—"

"Do *not*," Ethan said, snappish and heated. "It's a selkie—I *know* it's a selkie. A bullheaded, *ungrateful* selkie." He kicked uselessly at the shed. He was too far away to land a blow to the soggy wood, but he gave another kick for good measure.

"If you're right—"

"I *am* right!"

"*Whatever.* Just let it rest overnight. Coming back to life isn't exactly pleasant, trust me."

Ethan let his weight go heavy against Peter, breathed deeply, and gave a curt nod, resting the back of his head on his husband's collarbone. For the first time in three years, Peter Vásquez had admitted to dying. Indirectly, of course. But the statement still shocked through Ethan and turned his bones to jelly. "Fine, okay. I'm starving."

"You're also bleeding. C'mon, let's get you inside. We've got lasagna, don't we?"

"Yes, and butter lettuce from the garden. I'll make a salad."

"Okay," Peter said. His breath fogged the chilly air.

"Okay," Ethan echoed.

Neither of them moved for a while. They sat together in the misty garden, listening to the selkie shout and hoot.

CHAPTER TWO

E than stared at the ceiling, lulled by the sea but kept awake by thoughts of the selkie. The beast had gone quiet about an hour ago, its sad cries fading as they sat at the dinner table, picking at leftover lasagna and Caesar salad. Before that, Peter had lifted Ethan onto the countertop and taken his hand in a firm grip, tending to the shallow prick on his wrist with peroxide and bandages. It wasn't quite a cut, just a small puncture, but allowing Peter the opportunity to mend him put them both at ease.

They hadn't talked much. Ethan had been wading through the aftermath of the spell, his skull stuffed with cotton. Peter had been wise enough not to say *I told you so* and fixed them two servings each before retiring the empty pasta tray to the sink. Ethan had nursed a beer, which still sat half-empty on the nightstand, and Peter had taken a shower. He slinked into bed clean and freshly lotioned, lying on his side with his cheek cushioned on a lumpy pillow.

"You're insufferable, you know," Peter whispered.

Ethan's mouth ticked into a smile. "Isn't that why you married me?"

"I married you for your cooking, clearly."

"My *baking*. You and I both know I couldn't cook a proper meal if my life depended on it."

He laughed in his throat. "Right..." Peter hummed. "And you married me because I'm handy, is that it?"

"Oh, absolutely not. I married you for your looks, obviously," Ethan teased, turning to meet his eyes. Truth be told, it was for his heart. Because Peter was kind and good and humble, because he blushed like a raspberry whenever people looked at him for a little too long, because he'd loved Ethan Shaw fiercely since the day they'd met. "I'm handy enough for the both of us."

"Clearly. Bringing me back from the dead was a little showy though."

Ethan swallowed hard. *There*, he thought, *finally*. He watched Peter's rich, brown eyes soften and searched his face, waiting for the rest, for the truth.

"We've never talked about it," Peter said and cupped Ethan's jaw, thumbing tenderly at his cheekbone. "Was tonight some...some attempt at...at control? Some way to do it again, to make it happen on your own terms? Because—"

"Good Lord, Peter."

"Listen, okay? I know it takes a lot out of you. I know it's strenuous, but you don't need to prove—"

"*Anything*," Ethan interjected, snaring Peter in a hard glare. "What I did tonight was nothing like what I did to save you. It might look the same, and it might sound the same, but that night on the docks, I had no recipe, no spell, no ritual. I did something I can't replicate—*won't* replicate." Because it would likely kill him.

Would probably strip every bit of power from his bones. "That creature in our shed is alive because of a successful, safe ritual. You're alive because I could not fathom letting you go. Those are two very, *very* different things."

"Tell me how it's different."

"I would've bled every drop of magic to bring you back. I would've killed to bring you back. That selkie got a small taste of me; you were given the opportunity to take all of me. There's your difference, darling. If that botched ritual had called for a sacrifice, I would've slit the first throat within reach. Surely, you're aware I wouldn't do the same for a seal."

Peter's fine mouth tensed. He glanced around Ethan's face, tracing his coarse brow, the shell of his ear, and snaking his hand around the back of his head.

"So, it *is* a seal," he murmured, scuffing Ethan's lips with his scratchy beard.

"Shut up," Ethan said, but both syllables were muffled by a kiss. He seized Peter's jaw and kept him close, demanding to be kissed properly, deeply. For so long, they'd shared a bed, but despite familiarity, he still found himself surprised by the heat of Peter's breath, the way their teeth clumsily knocked, how his tongue moved sure and slow. Ethan opened his eyes mid-kiss and listened to the sound their lips made when they parted. "One day, I'm going to pack my things and find a sailor who appreciates me." He feathered his mouth across Peter's chin. "A good, quiet man who knows when he's wrong."

Chirped laughter filled the bedroom. "Well, only a fool would argue with you."

"Exactly."

Peter kissed him on the mouth and then the cheek.

They slept partially tangled, as they did most nights, with the ocean at their window, shushing and singing.

E very morning, Peter woke in the blue hour when night clung to the horizon and dawn gilded the sky. Sometimes, he slipped soundlessly from their bed—started the coffee, cracked the eggs, brushed his teeth. But typically, he stretched beneath wrinkled sheets and reached for Ethan. It was on those mornings that Ethan thought about children and legacies and names. Mornings when they fucked mindfully, like people who were *trying* fucked, like people who read magazines—*Make sure you're on your back! Elevate your legs! Stay connected after climax!*—fucked. On occasion, an orgasm would catch Ethan by surprise, rippling through him while Peter pinned his knees against the bed, widening him, making him accessible, gaping and open. But mostly, Ethan panted and stared at the ceiling. Waited for Peter to pull out, prop him on a pillow, fill his cunt with three fingers, and work him through a routine bout of bliss.

That morning, Peter suckled wetly at his clit. Ethan held on to the sensation, denying himself release until fingers bent, massaging his front wall, and Peter rolled his tongue, moaning against slick skin. He cupped Peter's buzzed head and cried out, gushing around calloused knuckles, hips jerking, stomach spasming. The pillow beneath him dampened. Sweat beaded on his flushed skin.

Ethan wanted to say *again*. Wanted to keep Peter home for the day. They could fuck like people who yearned for a child, and fuck like people who wanted each other, and fuck like they used to. The passion wasn't gone, per se, but Ethan missed who they'd been in the beginning. Insatiable and young and hungry.

Peter balanced on his free hand and lifted his face. "I bought some tea at the apothecary," he said. When he pushed away from the bed, the heel of his palm met Ethan's clit. He flexed his fingers. Slid one digit free and reached deeper. "Supposed to help with potency. Lady at the counter said lengthening our exposure time is our best bet. The longer my—" He cleared his throat. "—*I'm* inside you, the better our chances."

"I'm quite certain that's not how it works," Ethan said, catching his breath. He reached for Peter's wrist. Gripped around his pulse and trembled. "But I'm not opposed to keeping you here."

"I have to go," he murmured, nodding toward the window. He kissed Ethan gently. Pulled his hand free and rubbed downward, teasing at his back hole. "But I think it might be useful to buy a plug."

"You have a perfectly good plug between your legs."

"You know what I mean."

Ethan arched his hips, grinding against Peter's palm. "Stay. The boat can wait."

"The fish won't," he said and kissed him again. "I'll be home early, I promise. What should we have for dinner? Steaks, maybe? I can bring back a straggler if the catch is heavy."

"Pretty sure we still have bluefin in the freezer," Ethan mumbled. He watched Peter crawl away. Stared at his long, bronze torso, strong shoulders, and the dip where his tailbone curved inward. *We'd make beautiful babies.* Peter's handsome genes; Ethan's familial magic. But for three years, they'd had no luck. No *almost.* No *maybe.* Sometimes, on mornings when they tried, Ethan thought about Hurricane Katia, how he'd given himself over to a ritual he couldn't control, and wondered if their inability to create life was the payment. He tipped his knees toward his chest and rocked back and forth.

"How 'bout octopus, then?" Peter asked. He tucked an off-white shirt into black trousers and fastened the buttons on his ankle-length coat. "I'll bring home something fresh."

The floor wheezed under his socked feet. He appeared at their bedside again, blocking the muted light streaming in through the window.

"Ethan," he said gently, like he always did when quiet stretched too far between them. He took Ethan's chin between his fingers and forced his gaze. "What is it, *querido?*"

I miss you, Ethan wanted to say. *I've been missing you.* Instead, he said, "Worried about the selkie. That's all."

Peter furrowed his brow and tucked his mouth against Ethan's ear. "Te amo."

"I love you too," he said, sighing into a chaste kiss.

Peter doused his hands in the washroom, filled his thermos in the kitchen, and took a call on his way through the door. *Hello? Yes, I'll be there soon. Ready the crew.* Ethan listened to his voice carry through the window. He went limp atop the pillow and allowed his legs to sink. He stared at the pocked ceiling above their sturdy maple bedframe. Reached beneath his navel and covered himself, trapping the mess, and hoped it'd amount to something. He closed his eyes for a long time. Breathed. Settled into the effervescence that typically followed sleep. But before he could properly doze, he was startled by an incessant *buzz* on the nightstand. He snatched his phone.

Peter Vásquez: *Be careful with that seal.*

Ethan rolled his eyes, angled the screen between his thighs, and snapped a picture.

Ethan Shaw: *Should've stayed home <3*

He hit Send and silenced his phone, then stripped the case from the pillow, the sheets from the mattress, and trudged through the living quarters. He dumped the laundry into the hamper and himself into the shower. It was a heady type of missing when you missed a person you already belonged to. Loneliness knotted in his chest. He *had* someone. Loved someone. Honored vows with someone. But he missed the desire, missed being lusted after.

He snorted, scrubbing shampoo through his hair. *We aren't boring.* Two weeks ago, they'd coupled on the kitchen floor. On the summer solstice, when they'd argued in the lantern room, Ethan had pushed Peter against the domed glass and gone to his knees. They went down on each other in shared showers and made love on their anniversary. But Ethan missed the rest, the partnership that predated *trying* for something unattainable.

Not unattainable, he scolded and blew out a breath, jamming his toothbrush into his mouth. *Not impossible.*

They'd have a family one day. A beautiful, magical, handsome little family.

Ethan could—*would*—give Peter that.

He toweled off and walked naked through the lighthouse. In the bedroom, he dressed in another knit sweater and straight-legged denim. *That damn fae-beast'll need something to wear too.* He pawed through Peter's old clothes, searching for briefs and something warm—a crewneck sweatshirt and a pair of drawstring joggers. *And something to drink.* He paused in the kitchen and filled a mug with coffee. Added a sugar cube and stirred in fresh cream.

The selkie hadn't made a sound all morning. No banging, no trilling, no barking. Anxiety needled Ethan's throat. *What if it's dead, what if your power failed, what if you've depleted yourself, what if the magic left you.* He shooed the feeling and made his way to the shed, avoiding puddles left behind by midnight rain. Balancing the folded garments under his arm and the coffee in his palm, he eased the shed door open and braced for a corpse to greet him. Shadows filled the space, split by a streak of sunlight beaming through the shoebox-shaped window on the back wall. In the corner, huddled next to a sack of soil, the selkie peered at him.

"If you try to bite me again, I'll dump this on you," Ethan said, lifting the steaming mug. "It's volcanic."

The selkie, who hadn't taken human form, stretched its spotted head toward him and sniffed the air. A soft, chuffing noise rattled in its throat. It favored its left flipper, holding the limb close to its body. Ethan hadn't caught the scent of anything unusual last night, but right then, a pungent, coppery odor permeated the air. *Infection.* Like rancid oranges and sour meat.

"If you're hurt, I'll see to you..." He eased into the shed, hugging the adjacent wall, and set the clothes on the table.

The selkie didn't move, didn't make another sound, just kept its snout pointed toward him, watching.

Ethan wrinkled his nose. "I'm almost *certain* you're hurt, but if you'd rather go—" He set the coffee mug down. "—then be on your way. But I'd really like to take a look at—"

The selkie snapped its teeth.

Ethan jumped backward. "Right, then. Well, if you change your mind, I'm in the lighthouse. And fair warning, if you try to kill me, my husband will carve you into a new pair of boots. Understood?"

At that, the fae-beast tilted its head but stayed silent. Peter would *never*, but the stubborn-as-hell selkie didn't need to know that.

"Good. And speaking of skinning, I don't want your pelt if that's what you're worried about. I have zero interest in dealing with an indentured fae servant. Especially one as *friendly* as you, so—" He waved toward the table again. "—you're welcome."

Ethan resisted the urge to look over his shoulder as he left the shed, closing the door quietly behind him. No hooting followed. No trills or barks or growls.

He paused to dig up two sweet onions and cut a pumpkin off its thick, curly vine, allowing the selkie time to shift, maybe. To dress, appear, and speak to him. To do something, *anything*. Ethan waited and hoped the creature would come to its senses. But a particularly sharp wind skated his face, and he retreated inside, ducking to avoid another chilly strike.

Maybe the selkie wasn't a selkie at all. Maybe Peter had been right. Maybe Ethan had wasted his energy on a wild seal. *God forbid.*

Ethan rinsed the onions first. Thankfully, his magicked vegetables hadn't wilted. In spite of the wintery weather and bitter cold, Ethan's spell-work had kept his garden bushy and full. He took a knife to the hefty stem jutting from the gourd, sawed a hole in the top, and emptied seeds and guts into a colander. The shed never opened. No knock sounded at the door. After an hour had passed and Ethan had hollowed the pumpkin, sliced the onions, and boiled a pot of long-grain rice, he drummed his fingers on the counter and stared through the window behind the deep farm-style sink, watching seagulls swoop toward the water.

He was absolutely, no-questions-asked positive the creature—selkie or not—was hurt. Badly, if he had to guess. And if it wanted to swim, to survive, it'd need tending to.

"Stupid water dog," Ethan mumbled and rinsed his hands.

Not my problem, he reminded himself, repeating the statement as he stuffed the pumpkin with rice, goat cheese, tomatoes, rosemary, and onion. He banged around in the kitchen. Crushed thyme and basil in his mortar, nibbled a sharp cheddar square, poured a glass of seltzer, and huffed out a sigh. The grandfather clock across the room ticked. Another hour gone. *What now?* The weather hadn't changed enough to warrant re-logging for arrivals and departures, and the lantern was on an automated timer, scheduled to illuminate at dusk. Ethan only had one thing left to worry about. "Stubborn beast." He hated his achy, lonely heart. Hated *caring*.

"Well, I can't let you die again," he said to no one, to the selkie, to himself, and threw on his peacoat.

If he couldn't create life, he would damn well protect it. Or *try* to at least.

Brine chapped his cheeks. He pulled his collar upright and followed the path toward town, trudging through gravel and dirt until his heeled boots met cobblestone. The craggy coastline softened as he traveled inland. Gusty wind bent yellow grass, and smoke billowed from brick chimneys. A mule called to him, stretching over the fence at the Johansson farm. Bells clanked around cow necks, and chickens clucked in their coop. Wildflowers pushed through the fissures in the stone, and weeds climbed mailboxes.

Between dainty hills peppered with alder trees and hemlock, Casper appeared. There were square houses painted white, beige, and gray; little cars parked along the sidewalk next to scooters and bicycles; and boats easing into port and bobbing lazily at the docks. Tourists moseyed about as they always did, dipping into the Casper Brewery and browsing boutiques for Icelandic souvenirs. The locals bounced from the pub to the market, nursing cigarettes, manning registers, nannying children, mending nets. Like most coastal towns, Casper leaned toward the ocean, always damp, always creaky, always cold, and like most coastal towns, the folk held a bittersweet love for it. Like a thing they'd fixed, broken, and fixed again.

Ethan made for the herbiary, passing a booth stocked with Casper lilies—fake, of course—bundled in cellophane for naïve visitors. Specter Café boasted their signature maple mocha and sea salt taffy, scenting the air like coffee grounds and vanilla.

Miranda Park, who ran the metaphysical shop above Specter, waved from her balcony. "Afternoon, Ethan! Heard there's rain on the way. Stay warm."

"Good to see you," he said and threw her a smile. "Ah, well, of course there is. I left home, so it has to rain."

"*Of course*," she crowed, laughing. "Bring Peter over for dinner soon, all right? I'll make bibimbap!"

"Will do, Miranda. Take care!"

The Open sign glowed red in the herbiary's window, illuminating roses twined with burlap. Ethan gripped the door handle and snuck a glance over his shoulder. He caught a glimpse of the dark, swollen clouds rolling in from the sea and thought, *Peter*, as he always did when faced with a storm. He'd checked the weather though. The sea liked to spit at them, but not *every* storm was Katia. Still, he heaved a miserable sigh because rain—*of course, rain*—and walked inside. The bell above the door jingled. An orange tabby napped on a table stocked with beeswax candles, and the person behind the counter tilted their head, sweeping upturned eyes across Ethan.

"Ethan Shaw," they said, drawing his name between their teeth like syrup. "How can I help you?"

Ethan straightened in place, tugging at the bottom of his coat. "Have we met...?"

"Sure haven't. But I've heard the talk."

"The talk," he murmured, snorting defiantly. "And what *talk* have you heard?"

"That you're a witch. Seduced yourself a sailor. Whispered to his heart after it stopped beatin' and told it to start again. People say you got him under some kind of spell too." They purred, running their hand along the cat's back. "Got him hooked on you."

"Well, he's a captain, actually." Ethan browsed the shelves, collecting a jar of honey, powdered garlic, a bottle of apple cider vinegar, and dried orange peels. "But the rest is almost true."

"Which part? You sweet-talkin' his heart or him bein' hooked on you?"

"The former. Do you have eucalyptus?"

"I do." The clerk watched him. Inky curls framed their jaw, and their turtleneck sweater fanned open around a slender throat, ringed with cheap, gold chains. "Rumor has it you're tryin' for a baby."

Ethan wanted to throttle his senseless, trusting husband. "Rumor has it you shouldn't listen to apothecary gossip," he snapped lowly, like a wolf. He met their eyes, dark as night, and set the items on the counter. "Eucalyptus, please. Four ounces."

The clerk's thin mouth quirked into a smile. "Well, if that rumor is even *half*-true, I might be of assistance. Got myself a recipe for baby makin'. You know the kind, I expect."

Anger and shame twisted behind his belly button. He dug in his pocket, searching for his wallet. "I suspect I don't."

"From one witch to another, I'm sure you do."

He lifted his face, brows cinched, lips screwed into a snarl. "I haven't a clue what you're getting at but—"

"Easy." They reached beneath the counter and retrieved a glass vial filled with sallow liquid and held it between their thumb and index finger. "Harvested from the arctic. Narwhal, of course. Blended with consensually mined marrow. One teaspoon will last an entire night. Add to a drink or swallow straight. Doesn't matter."

Ethan stared at the vial. "*Marrow?*"

"Siren marrow." Their pierced eyebrow arched. "For encouragement. Voracity, if you will. You'll be irresistible to each other, and, well—" They cocked their head, considering. "—able to sustain for a much, *much* longer go."

Heat blistered in his cheeks. "I'm not sure we need—"

"Need is superficial. You want what this can give you, no?"

Ethan inhaled a shaky breath. In a primal, selfish way, he did. Reluctantly, he nodded.

They grinned, feline and coy, and held the vial out to him. "Take it, sweetheart. I'll get your eucalyptus. Full leaves, oil, or gel?"

"Leaves, thank you."

The syrupy substance slid along the glass. Narwhal teeth were particularly sought-after ingredients in witchcraft, but he'd never had the chance to see the material in person. He'd heard about foragers—witches diving into glacial water to scour the ocean floor for discarded tusks—but he'd never gone, and he'd never been privy to the treasure those witches returned with. Usually, alchemists, mystics, and magicians moved through Casper on their way to somewhere else. They came, traded, bartered, slept with sailors, stole lilies, and went on their way. Whoever this witch was, they were the first outsider to linger.

The clerk returned and set a pouch filled with leaves on the counter. Their long, equine face held a prettiness he hadn't noticed at first. Rich, umber-toned ochre skin. They tapped each item into the tablet-register and turned it around to face him. "Forty-three, please."

Ethan blinked. "That can't be right."

"Consider the marrow a gift. We're aware of each other now, no? And making someone's acquaintance can potentially lead to friendship." Beside them, the cat yawned, stretching its paws over the side of the counter. "People like us need friends."

He swallowed around an uncomfortable lump. "What's your name? I don't recall catching it."

"Lucia Belle." Their tone was disquieting. "It's a pleasure to finally meet you, Ethan Shaw."

"The pleasure's mine," he lied, then swiped his card, signed with his finger, and took the paper bag they'd meticulously filled. Forcing a tight-lipped smile, he made for the door, brushing past a giant monstera and macrame plant-holders.

"Good luck," they called. "That marrow calls for a light hand. Too much, and you'll be awake for days!"

Ethan acknowledged them with a jerky wave and shouldered through the door. Could his face get *any* hotter? If his damn husband hadn't blabbed to the gossipy she-devils at the apothecary, he would've gone to the herbiary, collected his supplies, and been on his way. But no. *No!* Of course not.

He kicked a rock and cursed under his breath. At the same time, thunder rumbled overhead. *Wonderful.* Ethan shoved the bag inside his coat and groaned, tucking his chin toward his chest as the sky opened, drenching Casper in quarter-sized raindrops. By the time he'd jogged back to the lighthouse, he was soaked. His socks squelched in the heeled Chelsea boots Peter had gifted him last Yule, and his binder clung to his skin. He tossed the bag onto the counter and stripped off his coat, leaving it piled on the floor with his sweater and pants.

"Marry a fisherman, Ethan. You've always loved being near the ocean," he mocked, almost toppling over as he peeled off his right sock, then his left. "Casper is such a *precious* town. Put down roots; make a life here."

Not that he'd ever leave Casper. Despite the terrible weather, nosey neighbors, and frosty climate, nowhere else would suit him half as well.

The front burner on the stove ignited. Ethan haphazardly lit the corner of a paper towel and threw the flame into the hearth, prodding it with skinny logs until the fireplace blazed. Rain kept falling, and waves grew, crashing against rocky cliffs. He shivered uselessly, still weighed down by his half-tank binder and sopping briefs. He stripped the rest of his clothes away, stepped into a pair of sweatpants, and put on one of Peter's long-sleeved shirts. Moth-eaten and old, the Henley slouched over his shoulders. He hadn't realized his phone was still in the pocket of his discarded jeans until the denim lit, glowing on the floor by the coatrack.

Peter Vásquez: *That's not fair*

Peter Vásquez: *omfg Ethan*

Peter Vásquez: *More?*

Peter Vásquez: *p l e a s e*

Peter Vásquez: *Okay c'mon*

Peter Vásquez: *You can't just send a dick pic and then stop respond-ing*

Peter Vásquez: *Babe please*

The next text was a picture taken from above. Peter's chest, his hand crammed inside his pants, the dirty tile in the tiny rig bathroom.

Peter Vásquez: *See what you did? Can't stop thinking about you*

Ethan grinned, pleased with himself.

Ethan Shaw: *I prepped dinner and went into town*

Ehtan Shaw: *Show me*

Three dots undulated in the text bubble. The next picture jolted through Ethan's groin. Peter, gripping himself, his cock hard and flushed, wet at the tip.

Ehtan Shaw: *Better hurry before someone calls for the captain*

Peter Vásquez: *Help me*

Peter Vásquez: *Please mi amor*

Ethan plopped on the floor and snapped several pictures, bend-ing his body into promiscuous poses. Some were okay; some were blurry. The two he chose were the best of the bunch. In the first, he arched, shirt pooled above his navel, tugging at the edge of his sweats. The second was a close-up of his mouth, two fingers curled behind his bottom teeth, tongue pink and wet, throat a dark chasm. He hit *send* and pushed to his feet. From the bag, he drew the vial of siren marrow and gave it a once-over. His phone lit on the countertop.

It was a video this time. Peter stroking himself, spurting over his knuckles, shaking and gasping. Ethan played it once, then turned up the volume and played it again, listening to Peter's shallow breath and muffled grunt. Heat pooled between his legs.

Peter Vásquez: *You're so fucking hot*

Peter Vásquez: *Be home soonish <3*

Ethan shifted his gaze to the vial. Maybe they didn't need it. Maybe all Ethan had to do was send a few pictures, get a little braver, and *ask* for what he wanted. He placed the marrow in the cupboard above the kettle and let it be. They could keep it for their anniversary. Or use it on a holiday—the longest night, maybe, when snow piled high against their door. Lick it off each other and fuck until sunrise. Watching his husband come apart in a cramped bathroom was enough to momentarily shoo his doubt. He played the video again, allowing his thoughts to drift, his eyelids to droop, his thoughts to wander.

It was the satchel of orange peels on the counter that brought him back to the present. To the wounded selkie, the unmade salve, the storm that would surely batter the poor thing if it tried to leave. He squeezed his thighs together and set his phone screen-down, focusing on the task at hand: caring for a damn fae-beast.

The salve was simple enough. Manuka honey bound the citrus, eucalyptus, garlic, and vinegar, and turned the mashed ingredients into a chunky paste. He dug spices out of the cupboard, added cloves, anise, and a dash of cinnamon. Stirred slowly. Leaning down, he murmured to the mixture. "To mend," he whispered, "to make whole." Lastly, he sent a glob of saliva into the bowl.

Witchcraft wasn't exactly cute. Spit, blood, semen, bone, flesh, hair. It always called for *something*.

Like pottery or pudding, the spell would take time to set. A few hours, maybe. He shuffled across the room, opened the door, and peeked out into the rain. The garden shed was firmly shut, but that didn't mean the selkie hadn't left. He hoped the mean, stubborn beast—whoever or *whatever* they were—was safely inside.

CHAPTER THREE

T he smell of tangy cheese, rosemary, and cooked pumpkin wafted through the lighthouse. Evening blanketed Casper, deepened by rain and blustery wind. Water streaked the window, and black reigned past the sharp cliffside, blotting out the gibbous moon and the many, many stars.

Ethan hated being stuck in weather like this, but he loved the atmosphere. The mood. He lit wicks stacked inside an iron candelabra in the center of the dining table. Tested the gourd in the oven with a fork. Lowered the needle on their ivy-green record player and hummed along to Bon Iver. He paid mind to the salve in the fridge as it turned from a yellowish mess into a mellow, near-translucent paste. It needed a few more minutes, just enough time for the magic to settle. Honey for healing; eucalyptus for cleansing; apple cider vinegar to eat away infection; cinnamon, garlic, cloves, and anise to detoxify; and orange peels to brighten the spirit. Hopefully, the selkie's wound wasn't as awful as it'd smelled. Ethan filled the kettle, placed it on a lit burner, and rested his palms on the edge of the counter.

It was then that Peter turned his key in the lock and entered, heaving a sigh. Ethan kept his eyes trained on the window. He watched candlelight warp Peter's reflection on the glass as he shrugged off his jacket, looped his scarf over a hook on the coatrack, and crossed the room in one, two, three long strides, aligning his chilly torso to Ethan's back.

"I brought an octopus," Peter said. He tucked his mouth against Ethan's neck. Pressed his lips there, beard scratchy and damp.

"Good. You'll grill it, then?" Ethan asked. Warmth seeped into his limbs. Embarrassment did too. There was nothing to be bashful about—Peter was his husband—but he hadn't sent a nude since he was twenty-two, probably. And he certainly hadn't been that forward with Peter since before Katia.

Peter hummed. "I will, yeah, after you tell me what got into you today." Playfulness filled his voice, paired with a strong grip on Ethan's hip and fingertips ghosting beneath his shirt. "They say ovulation can cause a spike in your sex drive—"

Ethan almost winced. "That's not—I mean, that's true, yes—but that's not..." He blew out an exhausted breath and eased away, sidestepping into the center of the kitchen. "Nothing got *into* me."

Peter frowned. "Is that right?"

"Yes, that's right," he insisted.

Peter frowned. He pushed his glasses up his nose. "Talk to me."

Talking was entirely necessary, but Ethan didn't know how to articulate the feeling wedged inside him. "I miss you," he said because it was the truth. "I miss being with you to *be* with you, not being with you to...to *try* for something."

Peter's expression immediately gentled.

"Please, don't—don't pity me, all right? I may not be able to carry a child, and I know that; I understand that. I don't want to give up, I just—"

"Ethan—"

"*Don't*," he said, rushed and breathy. "I just want to be wanted. I want...I want you to want *me* again. I know I'm running out of time; I know a pregnancy probably isn't viable, but—"

"You're twenty-nine," Peter blurted, exasperated.

"Twenty-nine and wondering if my husband still enjoys fucking me," Ethan snapped. His face flared hot. Something jagged lurched in his chest. That was the truth, wasn't it? A petty, squirming doubt he'd almost squashed earlier that day. Looking at Peter right then, studying his strong face and thoughtful gaze, Ethan felt it again—sandpaper on his rib cage, spines pricking his heart. "Well, okay, not exactly, but..."

Peter narrowed his eyes. His shoulders loosened, jaw slackened, and his mouth made the shape of the word *what* before he surged forward, steady on his feet, and crowded Ethan backward. Ethan held his breath when Peter took his wrists and caged them against the wall, holding him captive next to the pantry.

Peter leaned forward, speaking curtly into the space between their lips. "How long have you felt like this?"

Ethan's throat flexed. "A little while, I guess."

"*How long*?"

"I don't know, Peter. Long enough, all right? Since starting a family became a chore instead of a result of us being together. I know you want a child. I want to give you one, but—"

"I've loved you for a decade," Peter snapped, not unkindly. His expression softened, and he bumped his nose against Ethan's cheek. "Of course, I want a family, but for my husband, my partner in life, to think I... For you to think I don't *want* you...? Darling, that's unacceptable."

Darling. The timbre of his voice fluttered in Ethan's chest.

"We've been obsessed with trying, but I'm the one who keeps failing," Ethan whispered. The confession ran through him like a bullet. "We're always talking about new positions, new fertility tricks, and at first, it was okay—it's still okay—but it's heartbreaking when nothing works, when *I* don't work. I keep disappointing you—"

"No," Peter said, gripping his wrists tighter. "You've never disappointed me. When it comes to this, you can't disappoint me. It'll happen when it's meant to happen. No sooner, no later."

"And if it doesn't?"

"Then we'll buy an alpaca, or get a few dogs, adopt a rabbit. I don't know—I don't care. We'll have our family somehow, someway. But I need you to understand one very important thing." He released Ethan's right wrist and curled his hand beneath his jaw, framing Ethan's throat. "You're the only person I see, Ethan Shaw. I've wanted you since I was twenty years old—hardly a sailor, hardly a man, but entirely yours. I think about you *constantly*. Today I was..." He huffed out a laugh. "I was undone by you."

"Yeah, I saw," Ethan mumbled. He hadn't been held with such possessiveness in months. It set him ablaze.

"The next time you feel like this, fucking *tell* me." Peter tightened his hold just enough to shallow Ethan's breath. "I won't have an unsatisfied husband."

Ethan ran his hand along Peter's knuckles, clasped like a collar around his neck. "I'm sorry," he said because he didn't know what else to say. Here was his gorgeous, kind husband, demanding to know the inner workings of Ethan's insecurities. *I'm lucky*. He tipped his head, asking to be kissed. *I'm damn lucky*.

"Don't apologize," Peter mumbled and forced Ethan's chin upward, angling him where he wanted. Vulnerable, consumable.

Peter kissed him slowly. Pried at his slack mouth and sought him out, tongue dragging over his teeth, hot breath coasting into his throat. He kissed him deeply until their lips were wet, and Ethan's cheeks were horribly hot. Until Ethan was shaking with it—this *want* he'd hoarded like stolen goods—pushing against him, jerking his wrist free to clutch at Peter's clothes, his shoulder, his nape. Ethan moaned and whined, fumbling for Peter's obnoxious leather belt.

He wanted to go to his knees. Wanted Peter to lift him onto the counter. Wanted to be flipped around and railed, fucked, *taken*. Wanted to fill the bathtub and climb into Peter's lap, ride him in the hot water, say his name and hear it echo—

But the kettle whistled, and three heavy knocks sounded at the front door.

"Ignore it," Peter said.

Ethan whined, annoyed. "The kettle'll boil over, and—"

Another three knocks, louder, heavier.

"*Ignore it*," Peter said again.

"What if it's the selkie?" Ethan craned away, settling his gaze on the door.

"The *seal*?"

"It was hurt. Let me just... Just stay here—"

"Absolutely not. You stay here," Peter insisted, then stomped across the room.

Ethan followed at his heels, adjusting the too-big shirt and his loosened sweatpants. Desire snatched at the curiosity inside him, told him to keep the door locked, to yank Peter into the bedroom, to be selfish. But he couldn't. Not without knowing if the selkie had left, if it'd listened, if his magic had betrayed him or not.

Peter opened the door and turned on the porch lamp. Muted yellow light poured over muscular shoulders, illuminating a lean shape standing on their welcome mat. He wasn't quite as tall as Peter, but close. He wore the old gray joggers Ethan had left for him and shielded his left side with crossed arms. Relief unspooled inside Ethan, accompanied by a short gasp.

"I can't swim," the selkie said breathlessly. Water dripped from his nose and fell from his auburn hair. He said it again, growlish and desperate. "I—I *can't* swim like this."

Peter tilted his head. "Excuse me, but—"

"Of course, you can't," Ethan said. "You're hurt, aren't you? I knew it. C'mon, get inside."

"Who *are* you?" Peter asked.

"Nico," the selkie said at the same time Ethan said, "The goddamn *seal*."

Peter adjusted his glasses and blinked, glancing between the pair.

Nico crept inside. He was barefoot and almost human. The webbing between his toes and fingers said otherwise, as did the faint spots flecked on his clavicles and printed on his torso. But still, he was acutely handsome, strong jawed, wide-mouthed, and well-built. His eyes were dark pits, flashing the faintest brown in the candlelight.

"Don't bite me," Ethan said, almost teasing. *Almost.*

Nico stood beside the kitchen table, shifting his gaze awkwardly around the room. "Don't reach into my mouth then."

"Well, I didn't really have a choice seeing as you were *dead*, but it's lovely to know you can talk." Ethan filled a bowl with water from the kettle, retrieved the salve from the refrigerator and bandages from underneath the sink. He pointed at the washroom, speaking to Peter. "Grab some towels, please."

Peter didn't move at first. He stared at Nico, assessing him like an adversary.

"Sit," Ethan said and gestured from Nico to a chair. He raised his brows at Peter. "*Please.*"

Nico sat, and Peter went, and Ethan thought he might vibrate out of his skin. Not because Nico was beautiful—*he was*—but because Ethan had done it. He'd succeeded. And it wasn't until he came to stand in front of Nico that he remembered his lightweight shirt, how he was wearing nothing beneath his sweats, and had to convince his body not to go rigid.

"Do you know what happened?" Ethan asked, clearing his throat.

Nico watched him through his lashes the same way an animal would. Not prey—predator. "I was pulled under by a riptide, got caught in a net, and hit a reef." He uncurled his arms and flinched, hissing through his teeth. Beneath his left bicep, a gash yawned open on his rib cage. The deep puncture didn't bleed, but the flesh was raised and sallow, reddened around the edges and raw within. Infection seeped from the wound, pushed outward by a body desperate to survive. "It's not that bad."

"You're right, it's awful," Ethan corrected. He wrinkled his nose and tipped his head from side to side, cataloging the nasty fissure. "But I can fix this, I think. You'll be landlocked a week. Maybe two."

"Landlocked?"

"If you don't give yourself time to heal, this'll get worse. Keeping it dry and clean are the first two steps, letting it close enough to stitch is the third."

Peter set two towels on the table. He moved cautiously, body held on a tripwire. "Nico, was it?"

The selkie lifted his chin, tracking Peter as he moved through the kitchen. "Yeah, Nico Locke."

Ethan turned to look over his shoulder. "Will you pull the pumpkin out of the oven and fix that octopus?" He swiveled back to Nico. "Speaking of which, when's the last time you ate?"

Nico flared his nostrils. His flighty gaze flicked around. "It's been a minute."

"What's a selkie of your..." Peter hummed, considering. "Breed feels like the wrong word. Kind, I suppose. What's a selkie of your kind doing this far south?"

Nico didn't answer. His eyes moved quickly, and his knuckles whitened in his lap. He stayed eerily still, shivering on the wooden chair.

Ethan soaked a towel in the hot water. "This might sting," he said, an uncertain warning, and pressed the wet fabric to Nico's side.

Nico flinched and bared his teeth, sucking in a sharp, audible breath.

"I'm sorry—I know," Ethan blurted and inched closer, sealing the towel over the wound. "This is the worst part, all right? But I need it clean."

Everything—the air, the storm, the three of them—seemed strung between fight and flight. Peter made a worried noise, and Ethan scanned the selkie's pinched face as Nico clutched the side of the table. But no one attempted to do anything other than what needed to be done. Peter took the pumpkin out before it burned, and Ethan dabbed at the gash until it stopped oozing, and Nico gritted his teeth. Once it was over, it was over. The towel hit the floor, Nico caught his breath, and Ethan thanked whatever god might've been listening for avoiding the selkie's teeth.

"The salve might be uncomfortable to apply, but it'll feel better after it's on," Ethan said.

"What is it?" Nico stared at the bowl on the table. Before Ethan could answer, he asked, "Who are you?"

"I'm Ethan Shaw. That's my husband, Peter Vásquez, the man who pulled you ashore and brought you here."

"I suppose it was *your* net, then?" Nico mumbled. He settled into the seat and stretched his legs, allowing his shoulders to drop. His attention was fixed on Peter.

Peter slammed a wide-handled knife through three tentacles. He met Nico's gaze. "It was."

Nico lifted his chin. Confidence came off him in waves, battling with the exhaustion purpling his eyes and the slight tremor in his hands. For a moment, Ethan thought he might've made a mistake, might've invited a territorial, vengeful creature into their home, but neither Peter nor Nico bristled or taunted. They did what most men tended to do—frowned, stared, and waited.

Ethan leaned backward, glancing between them. "Anyway, I'm his partner—hello, again—yes, me, the one who breathed life into your lifeless body." He gave a sarcastic, little wave. "Peter happens to captain a fishing rig, and you happened to swim into his net. And by the good grace of Hecate, he happens to have a witch for a spouse. So, let's all take a breath and be thankful to know one another."

Peter raised his brows and gestured to Ethan with the slimy knife as if to say, *He's right.*

Nico Locke shifted his jaw back and forth. "What is it?" he asked again, jutting his chin toward the bowl.

The tension seemed to dissipate. *Landmine avoided.* Ethan sighed and gave a curt nod. "A salve imbued with a healing spell. Organic, obviously. Nothing out of the ordinary."

"And you had it on hand for...?"

"You," he said, tempering the heat in his voice. "I noticed you were hurt earlier, as I'm sure you remember, and I collected the ingredients in case you decided to stay."

Candlelight gilded Nico's upper half, chasing shadows across his olive skin. He assessed Ethan skeptically but didn't move away when Ethan scooped the salve onto his fingers. Ethan spread the mixture as carefully as he could, paying mind to Nico's stuttering breath and clenched abdomen.

"Did you try to leave in this?" Ethan shrugged toward the window. Rain pelted the glass. Lightning winked across the waves.

Reluctantly, Nico nodded.

"Well, don't do that again. Not unless you're on a boat or stitched up."

"You can stay here," Peter said. The octopus popped on a griddle, perfuming the room with lemon and black pepper. "We've got a rollout cot and extra blankets. You'll have access to a shower, food, everything you need."

After their previous stint of dreadful silence and aggressive eye contact, Ethan had expected Peter to fix their plates, place the cot on the floor, and retire to their bedroom without another word. But of course, Peter was generous. Of course, he was kind. He always had been. Ethan was sure he always would be.

"I can find other accommodations," Nico said briskly. He searched the floor, brows pulled together in concentration. "If it's...if it's trouble, I'm sure I could—"

"It's no trouble," Ethan said, halfway to a whisper, and shot Nico a narrow glance. "Stay, heal, rest for a while." When Nico opened his mouth to interject, Ethan blurted, "We insist," and grabbed a roll of bandages.

Nico pursed his lips and stayed quiet.

The storm raged. Peter plated their dinner and uncorked a bottle of cranberry wine. Ethan wrapped the clean, white bandage around Nico's chest, secured it with a metal clip, and took the dirty tools to the sink. Once the leftover salve was transferred into an airtight container, Ethan gave Nico a clean bath towel and sat at the table. Like this, patched together and scrubbing seawater from his skin, Nico Locke appeared far younger than he had on their doorstep. He was wildly handsome—long lashed and fierce, oddly built and tightly held.

Ethan rested a stemless glass on his bottom lip. He studied the markings on Nico's chest, the blotchy spots reminiscent of his seal pelt. Wine sloshed against his mouth, and he said, "Peter asked you a question earlier. Where are you from?"

Peter kept his face relaxed, elbows resting atop the table, socked foot bumping Ethan's ankle beneath the table. He sipped his beer—frosty bottle seated beside his wine glass—and tilted his head, saddling Nico with a questioning look. Double-fisting two separate libations probably, *definitely*, informed his raised guard.

"North," Nico said. The fork looked obscure in his hand, propped against the translucent webbing between his thumb and index finger. He brought a piece of pumpkin to his mouth. Chewed. Swallowed. "Obviously, my *kind* are typically found in the Arctic." He leveled Peter with an annoyed glare. "But my colony migrated to a more hospitable climate once the glacier run-off became too fast and unpredictable to manage. Some of us are in Alaska, others in Ireland. A few made homes in Norway. I'm not mated, so I tend to wander. I have an aunt in Reykjavík which is what brought me to these parts."

"Reykjavík is quite a long swim from Casper," Ethan said.

"It is. But I'd heard the stories about the mystical Casper flowers. Wanted to see for myself what this island had in store." Nico shrugged. He shifted his gaze to Ethan and then to his plate.

"Stories," Ethan echoed bitterly. He finished his wine in one go and poured another glass. "Yeah, I guess we're rife with those 'round here."

After that, no one spoke.

Peter toyed with his food for a while, picking at charred tentacles and cooked cheese. Ethan poured more wine, earning a suspicious glance from his husband, and Nico cleaned his plate. It was strange, sharing the silence with a man who'd always fit into his life like an organ, and a man who'd wandered into their home like a leak or a bear—capable of causing invisible damage or very real, very visible problems. That was the messiness, wasn't it? The consequence that came with magic as intimate as necromancy. That both Peter Vásquez and Nico Locke carried a bit of Ethan with them. His magic, his lifeforce. The power in Ethan's blood would call to itself from where it'd rooted in their bodies, a ripple traveling backward toward its source.

Ethan had torn Peter away from the reaper. He'd sweet-talked water from his lungs and made a sacrifice he couldn't name. But Nico's reanimation was a calculated kind of magic. A ritual he'd followed step by step, piece by piece. Dazed and trapped in thought, he took the dishes to the sink and ran the faucet.

Maybe Peter was right. Maybe Ethan had brought the selkie back to prove something to himself. That he *could*. That his blood didn't have to cost quite as much as it had the first time. But now, he was inexplicably tied to the man he'd taken vows with and, somehow, to a stranger too. Vulnerability knotted in his gut. The same kind that came after babies were born, bankruptcies were filed, and divorces were penned. Regret, relief—both.

"Feel free to whatever we have in the fridge," Peter said, shattering the silence. "If you need more blankets, they're in the linen closet." His hand closed around Ethan's wrist. "C'mon, we'll finish that in the morning."

Ethan stole a glance over his shoulder. He hadn't expected to find Nico watching him, but the selkie sat unmoving at the dining table, lit by waning candles, tracking him with dark, amber eyes. He slouched in the chair, lips parting, as if he had something to say. Nico closed his mouth, and Ethan looked away. Peter's warm, wide hand settled on his tailbone, and their bedroom door wheezed on its hinges, shutting behind him.

CHAPTER FOUR

The storm stayed.

Thunder cracked, rain fell, and Ethan hardly slept. He let his gaze wander, scanning the hamper, the crowded dresser, a photo-strip pinned to the wall. The wine cushioned him. It kept him woozy and dazed, acquiescing to thoughts of Nico, Peter, and magic. Life, death, and children. Lightning blinked through the bedroom window, and he noticed Peter beside him—those pretty eyes cracked open, lashes casting thin shadows along his cheekbone.

"Can't sleep?" Peter rasped.

Something akin to regret—shame, maybe—swelled inside him. Ethan turned onto his side, whispering into the space between them.

"I haven't been unsatisfied," he said. Not exactly the truth, not false enough to be a lie. "And I'm not...I'm not at a loss, but I don't know how much hope I have left to spare. I need to refill my well. Stop thinking about it for a while."

Peter brushed his knuckles along Ethan's jaw. He was quiet for a while, nodding gently, staring at Ethan's mouth. He clucked his tongue and finally said, "How could you possibly think I don't enjoy you?"

Oh. Ethan parted his lips, but nothing followed. No explanation. No excuse. Sadness ballooned in his chest, airy and familiar and too big to ignore. *Because I'm unwantable. Because I'm barren.*

"Because I've failed you," he croaked, and for the first time since they'd said *yes, a family; yes, let's try,* Ethan cried. He hiccupped and sniffled, sucked in little gasps and shook. He hadn't shed a tear after any of the four, five, six wasted pregnancy tests, hadn't trembled in his paper smock at the fertility clinic, hadn't cried alone when he'd stayed in bed, hips elevated, staring blankly at the ceiling. But that night, his mouth wobbled, his lungs ached, and he simply fell apart.

"No," Peter said desperately and pressed his lips to Ethan's forehead, his temple, his cheek. "You haven't. You *haven't.*" He brought Ethan closer, curving around his smaller frame, giving patient assurances. "Of course not. No, mi querido."

Once the floodgates opened, there was no stopping it. Ethan babbled, spouting ridiculous things. Untrue things. *I'm sorry; I wouldn't blame you if you left me; this is what you get for marrying a witch; I'm fruitless; you deserve better.* The pillow under his cheek grew damp. His face surely reddened, and his throat became tight and chalky.

How was there this much pain in loss he hadn't experienced yet? How could the absence of something—a child he'd never carried—even constitute as loss? He couldn't pinpoint an answer. Couldn't logically find a reason for such deep, unrelenting grief. But Peter held him, as he always did, and he whispered against his skin, as he tended to do, and he loved Ethan fiercely, as he had for a decade. Ethan folded against Peter's chest and hid there, seizing through trapped sobs and ugly gasps.

"Te amo," Peter whispered, "te amo, te amo," like a chorus in the dark room.

Ethan didn't remember falling asleep. But at some point, he must've because he woke to an echo of that *te amo* ghosting through their silent bedroom. Sunlight warmed the floorboards, and seagulls screeched, scouring the shallows for fish displaced by the storm. He faced the window, lying on his side with Peter still curved around him, a protective crescent tucked against his back. He pawed at his clumped lashes and inhaled deeply, thankful for the rest, thankful for the release too. Crying was something he actively avoided. He'd go red-faced and glassy-eyed, but he'd never cry. Not like that. Not like someone who'd lost something.

The last time he'd wept, he'd knelt over his drowned husband, raking a ritual out of thin air. This time, the emptiness left him elated.

Peter woke quietly. His breathing shallowed, and he dragged his fingertips over Ethan's forearm, sharing the stillness.

"Do you remember our wedding night?" Peter asked.

Ethan laughed in his throat. "Of course, I do."

"You were aggressively drunk."

"I was marginally tipsy."

"A whole mess."

"Hardly," Ethan whispered, snorting. "Remember when you pushed me into the bathtub? Awful brute."

"*Pushed you*? Please. My graceful, brand-new husband sat on the edge of the garden tub in our honeymoon suite and fell backward."

"You poured champagne on me," Ethan whispered, wading through a faraway memory. They'd married inland, under a blackberry bramble during a hot, humid summer. Miranda Park had wrapped their hands in red thread, told them to sip from a chalice filled with honey wine, and officiated their union. They'd danced and drunk and laughed until sunset. "Carried me to bed too."

"You asked me to go slow." Peter nosed at his throat. Opened his mouth over Ethan's pulse and worried his heartbeat. "Told me to make it last."

He pushed his hips backward, fitting his ass against Peter's crotch. "Is that right?"

Peter toyed with the elastic band on Ethan's briefs. "Thought you remembered."

"Remind me," he said on a sigh. Desire brewed behind his belly button.

The morning lingered.

Ethan craned his neck, making room for Peter's teeth. Closed his eyes and allowed himself to be pliant. Languid and usable. Peter laid heavy, purposeful touches on him—stroked his slit, mouthed at his shoulder, turned him onto his belly. Ethan clutched the pillow under his cheek. His blush deepened as Peter pulled his knees upright, palms trailing Ethan's inner thighs, breath hot between his legs, coarse stubble a shock to his skin.

Sometimes Ethan remembered being bashful. A long, long time ago, he would've whimpered at the suggestion of a position like this—laid bare and on display in a sunlit room. But age and time and togetherness had made him crave it. The vulnerability, the openness. He closed his eyes and endured the rising heat pressing on the underside of his skin, stoked by Peter licking into him, dragging his tongue over slick folds, higher, probing at his rim.

He muffled weak noises against the comforter, quivering in the space just after waking. The time when everything was soft and buoyant and raw. Peter gripped the back of his thighs and spread him, mouth hungry and slow, guiding Ethan over the edge of a deep, fluid orgasm. His abdomen flexed, and his cunt spasmed. He clawed at the bed, whining into a pillow, rocking backward and forward until Peter gripped his hips and held him steady, working him through the natural high, the unrelenting pulse in his groin, the aftershocks that left him dizzy.

Yeah, I've missed this.

Peter smeared his messy lips along Ethan's spine and kissed his nape. "Been thinkin' about that picture you sent me. Your smart fuckin' mouth," he murmured.

Ethan gazed over his shoulder, breathing hard. "How do you want me, then?"

"On your knees," Peter said, like a command, like someone Ethan had known years ago, back when they were young and fucking in dive bar bathrooms, on the bridge of his ship, anywhere they could.

His limbs were jumpy and half-numb, so Ethan said, "Put me there," and kissed Peter, chasing the taste of himself on his slick mouth.

He hummed when Peter lifted him by his waist and shifted clumsily as Peter slid off the bed and guided him closer, easing one foot onto the floor, then the second.

Peter kissed him deeply, but the tiniest pressure on his shoulders sent Ethan to his knees, chin tipped upward, eyes half-curtained, and the slightest part of his lips sent Peter into his space, cock filling his mouth on a single, ill-restrained thrust. Ethan hadn't prepared for the suddenness. Hadn't expected his throat to rebel, flexing—roughly, wetly—around Peter. Hadn't expected Peter to gasp and moan and grip the back of his skull. His eyes watered and stomach jumped, jaw loosening for a noisy gag. It'd been forever since they'd fucked like this. Like people who wanted to use each other. Be used by each other. Ethan swallowed around him. Saliva coated his lips and greased his chin, and he blinked, flinching as he stared at Peter, memorizing his husband's blotchy face, knitted brows, parted mouth. Peter came quickly. Snapped his hips and ran his fingers through Ethan's hair, holding him against his pelvis until he squirmed. Ethan swallowed what he could. Choked a little, eyes blurred by hot tears, and eased away to breathe.

Peter stared down at him, chest heaving, bathed in the crisp morning light. "You okay?" he asked and wiped wetness from the corner of Ethan's swollen mouth.

Ethan subconsciously touched his throat. "Ouch," he mumbled, nodding. He tasted salt and skin, felt sated and hollow. "But, yeah, I'm fine—help me."

He lifted his arms. Peter took his wrists, then his elbows, and hoisted him to his feet. He held Ethan's face between his palms and thumbed his lips, an odd, intimate thing, touching where he was wrecked and overworked.

"Was I too rough?" Peter asked.

"No—*almost*, you were quite close—but no."

Peter furrowed his brow. "You're a hot mess," he said, swiping moisture from his face, and then kissed him sweetly. Such a Peter thing to do. Roughen him in one breath and hold him tenderly in the next. "Come wash up with me? I'll put the kettle on too." He made a move to step away, but Ethan stopped him.

"There's a selkie in our living room, dear. I don't think we can waltz through the kitchen like this."

"Right," Peter blurted, glancing at himself. His blush worsened.

How dare you be shy with me after that, Ethan thought and smiled, *you ridiculous man.*

"A robe, at least," he whispered, pressing his lips to Peter's again. "Underwear, maybe."

They shuffled around the room. Ethan put on socks, flannel pajama pants, and a sweatshirt. Peter dressed in his knee-length robe. He looked older right then, silver catching in his dark, coarse beard.

In the living quarters, penny-colored kitchenware glinted on the wall, and wax cooled underneath the candelabra on the table. Nico slept with his back turned to them, balled like a cat on the floor-cot. His toes peeked out from the blanket, nose hidden, body tilted toward the hearth. Ethan hadn't noticed the scar on the back of his neck. Like a knot, the bundled flesh twisted, reminiscent of a burn. *His pelt,* he thought and almost tripped following Peter into the kitchen. *That's where his pelt was first snipped.* Like most fae creatures, selkies had a place of attachment, a key where their otherworldliness met the human plane. Their pelt was that key: a thing clipped, carried, and protected. In the wrong hands, a selkie's pelt could cost them their life or even their freedom; whoever held the pelt controlled the beast. If they died in their human skin, no spell could undo it.

Ethan tore his eyes away from Nico and tiptoed to the washroom. Peter put the kettle on and joined him, locking the door. He pulled Ethan into a steaming shower and kissed him against the tiled wall. They soaped each other, and Ethan laughed as he scrubbed his sudsy fingers on Peter's buzzed head.

"Should we talk about last night?" Peter asked.

Ethan's heart floundered. He swallowed around anxiety. "No," he said, cutting at first, then softer, "no, I'd rather not if that's okay."

"As long as *you're* okay."

"I... I am. I will be," he said, and again, "I will be."

Peter had eyes like a Labrador or a golden retriever. Big gentle eyes framed by girlish lashes. He could never harden them. Not at sea, not at home. Even in anger and worry, his eyes were brown sugar. Warm and syrupy and readable. Those same eyes had looked back at him since they were boys—since he'd hardly known he *could* be a boy—and he knew the hurt splintered behind them.

"I promise," Ethan added, nodding. Steam rose around them, and soap circled the drain at their feet. He laid his hand on Peter's chest and forced a smile.

"I'll always take care of you," Peter murmured and tapped his index finger on Ethan's temple, "here," dropped his hand to his sternum, "here," slipped lower, cupping his palm between Ethan's legs, "especially here. Understood?"

"*Especially.*" Ethan huffed out a laugh, then blushed and batted Peter's hand. "Enough of that, we'll be in here for hours. Go check the kettle—*go.*" He swatted away another playful touch to his rear and stepped out of the shower, snatching a fluffy towel.

Peter dried off, tied his robe, and halted in the doorway. "Oh," he said, cocking his head. "You're awake."

Ethan peeked around his husband's wide frame and saw Nico adjusting the drawstring on his borrowed sweatpants.

"I am." Nico straightened his shoulders. "I don't know where you keep your tea, but I took the kettle off."

"In the cabinet," Peter said, pointing to a cabinet neatly labeled with a cursive sign Tea & Coffee. He arched a brow. "How long were you a seal?"

"*Peter*," Ethan hissed and smacked his arm.

Nico pushed air through his teeth. "A while. Look, hey," he said, almost barking, and met Ethan's eyes. He plucked at his bandages. "These itch. Really itch. Like, *bad*—"

"Well, don't scratch it," Ethan snapped. He moved around Peter and swung his arm toward the kitchen. "Can you handle the tea?"

Peter frowned.

"Or *I* can fix the tea while Nico enjoys the beginning stages of sepsis. Your call, love."

This time, Nico frowned.

"You're dramatic," Peter said, his curtness almost coy, and made for the stove.

"And you're petty—Nico, come here; sit down." Ethan pulled out a chair and waited for him to sit, then unfastened the clips and eased the bandages away. When they pulled at his skin, Nico made an inelegant noise, like a hiss but deeper. Ethan almost shrank, but he steadied his hands instead. "Sorry. I know... I can't imagine how uncomfortable this is... There we go." He squinted at the wound. "Okay, not sepsis."

Nico curled his top lip. "Great. What is it, then?"

"Healing hurts sometimes; bodies sweat, sweat itches—you see where I'm going. I'll clean this and reapply the salve. Not to be a downer, but after that, you'll have to let it be for a while. As in no itching—"

"I'm not an idiot. I heard you," Nico bit out. Despite his tone, the selkie looked far from angry. Upset, yes. But more so, he appeared stranded. Lost, almost. His throat flexed—a whole damn show—and he parted his lips, fumbling for something to say. "I'll cook. I *can* cook, I mean. Tonight. If you'd like." He paused, glancing between Ethan and Peter. "I'm sorry for barking at you. That was rude."

"It was," Peter quipped.

"Ignore him," Ethan said. "But you do bark a lot."

"What kind of tea do you have?" Nico asked. He lowered his voice politely.

Before Ethan could answer, Peter said, "Loads. Peppermint, chamomile, oolong, caravan black tea, Earl Grey, rose verbena. Take your pick. There's coffee too."

Nico leaned forward. He craned his neck, one arm propped over the back of the chair, allowing his wound to air out, and wiggled his nose. A very seal thing to do. "Earl Grey, please. With milk if you have it."

Ethan retrieved the salve from the refrigerator and filled a bowl with lukewarm water. "Peppermint for me."

Through the window, gray skies reigned, cloaking the sun and turning the town varying shadowy shades. The fireplace still burned, and the smell of sourdough wafted from the toaster, accompanied by soaking tea leaves, sweet butter, and the salty scent tossed in from the tide. Ethan pulled a chair up to where Nico sat and dabbed the puncture with a damp towel then scooped the salve onto his fingertips and applied it.

"Sorry; I know it's cold," Ethan mumbled, spreading the ointment over pinkened skin.

He lifted his face and met Nico's eyes. The selkie was flushed—from discomfort, of course—and chewed his bottom lip. Ethan stayed there for a fraction too long, looking at Nico, Nico looking back, and ducked away once the *clank* of a mug banged on the table.

"Do you take sugar?" Peter asked.

Nico stammered. "W-what?"

Ethan stole another glance and caught Nico with his chin tipped upward, flushed, vulnerable, staring at Peter. That was an aspect of the situation Ethan hadn't considered until right then: Nico Locke being extraordinarily compromised. He couldn't fight, couldn't leave, couldn't do a damn thing. If they wanted to, Ethan and Peter could've taken his pelt, or sold him to a fae trader, or hurt him worse. If Nico had landed somewhere, anywhere else, that's the future he might've faced.

Instead, he'd been caught in Captain Vásquez's net—a man who would mistake a selkie for a leopard seal, drag the poor thing home, and cry when it refused to wake up.

"For your tea?" Peter clarified, tilting his head curiously.

"Oh, no, thank you," Nico said.

Peter dropped a sugar cube in the minty mug and slid it toward Ethan. He set a carton of milk down for Nico, then knuckled his tea across the table too. "There's toast and butter on the counter. I need to get ready for work," Peter said and took Ethan's chin between his fingers, steering him into a quick kiss.

There was no need to blush. Peter was his husband for Christ's sake. But Ethan's cheeks still blistered, and he still cleared his throat, nodding as Peter balanced a piece of toast atop his mug and carried it into the bedroom. He avoided Nico's gaze. Unrolled a fresh bandage and wrapped it around his spotted chest.

"I can do it," Nico said.

Ethan almost startled. He kept the bandage in place while Nico took it. His chair made an awful noise when he scooched backward.

"I'll leave you to it, then." He curled two fingers through the handle on his mug, followed Peter, and closed the door behind him. "Why're you weird around him?" Ethan aggressively sipped his tea. The peppermint soothed his sore throat.

"*Weird*? I'm not weird," Peter said, hushed and low. He shot Ethan a narrow-eyed glance. "*You're* weird."

Ethan gaped at his half-dressed husband. "I am *not*. You've been nothing but passive-aggressive and cagey with Nico since he got here. What's going on?"

Peter huffed, tugging a thick-knit beanie over his ears. His cheeks darkened, and his mouth squirmed, eyes darting around the floor.

Oh. A laugh tumbled off Ethan's lips. "You're jealous," he hissed, grinning like an imp. "You're jealous of a lost selkie *you* fished out of the ocean. Is that it? Oh, darling, oh my God. You sweet, stupid man—"

"I am *not* jealous. He's just *very* handsome," Peter snapped. "Admit it, he is."

"I have eyes, Peter. Of course, he's handsome. But c'mon, really?"

"I'm leaving a wild fae-man with my husband who recently revealed his dissatisfaction in the bedroom. I think I'm allowed some discomfort, no?"

"You keep going back to that, don't you? I am satisfied; I'm just tired of putting *us* aside to chase something I haven't been able to... to produce." Ethan set the mug on the dresser and rested his wrists on Peter's shoulders. "A *very* handsome—your words, not mine—selkie shouldn't be a reason for you to question my faithfulness."

"I don't question you; I question myself," Peter said, sighing.

"There's no need to. You know I'd never."

"I know," he murmured, leaning his forehead against Ethan's. "But he's running around shirtless in my house, flaunting his Irish skin, all surly and mysterious. I've seen the way you look at him."

"I've seen the way *you* look at him," Ethan countered. "And I could care less about his skin. I prefer my men with a deeper complexion, anyway." He brushed his knuckles across Peter's brown cheek, smoothing a piece of his short beard into place. "Colombian, specifically."

"Is that so, brujito?"

Little witch. Ethan smirked. "Yeah, it's true."

Peter made an unsure noise and kissed him. "Make him put a shirt on."

"I doubt I can *make* him do anything."

Another uncertain noise, similar to a cat's growl. "Well, give him one at least. And be careful, all right? We don't know him."

Ethan hummed. "Yeah, yes, okay. Be safe on the boat. Turn back if the storm isn't through."

"Looks clear enough." Peter paused in the doorway. He shrugged on his coat, wrapped a scarf around his neck, and darted a glance at Nico. "I have extra clothes if you need it. Might not be a perfect fit, but..." He shrugged, nodding toward the bedroom. "They'll keep you warm."

"Appreciated." Nico stood in front of the sink with a mug clasped between his big hands. His chest was clumsily bandaged, and his bare toes curled and uncurled against the floor. He steered his attention from Peter to the window.

Peter slid another worried glance to Ethan before he left, letting in a burst of chilly wind as he pulled the front door shut.

Logs popped in the fireplace, the ocean roared outside, and quiet filled the lighthouse. The wood floor creaked under Ethan's slow footsteps. He buttered a slice of toast, spooned a dollop of honey onto its center, and took a bite, staring at the scar on Nico's nape.

"Are you okay?" Nico asked, far too softly.

Ethan stopped chewing. "Yeah," he slurred, unsurely, and waited for Nico to turn around.

He stayed still, though, staring at the ocean through the dewy window. "You were crying last night."

"I... No, I—"

"I heard you, necromancer. I have good ears."

"Fine, well, it's not your concern," he said, mouth stuffed with sweet bread. *What else did you hear?* He ran hot beneath his clothes.

Nico tipped his chin, looking at Ethan over his shoulder. "Your husband didn't mention that tea," he said and slid his eyes toward the tins and satchels next to the kettle.

A paper bag labeled Fertili-Tea sat next to the peppermint container. The corner was torn, and someone had drawn a smiley face on the front. One of those vulturous, gossiping she-devils from the apothecary, no doubt. Ethan stuffed the rest of the toast into his mouth. Chewed, swallowed, and licked honey from his lips.

"Are you worried about your potency?" Ethan asked, a saccharine hiss, and dropped his gaze to Nico's waist.

The corner of Nico's mouth twitched upward. He snorted, a sound typically paired with offense or sarcasm. "Not particularly."

"Then he didn't need to mention it."

"How long have you been trying?"

"That's none of your business."

"And you think tea'll help? A floral blend? That's your cure?"

"I think you're being very brave," Ethan snapped.

Power surged outward, reaching from behind his bones. It was unusual for magic to build inside him on accident, to make itself known without explicit intent. But whatever he carried with him—whatever ancestral energy and leftover otherworldliness he'd kept hidden—caused the fire to dim, the lights to flicker, the kettle to give a short shout. He hardened his expression. Guarded himself against the shame swelling in his core.

Nico's wry smirk dropped. "I'm sorry. I didn't mean—"

"Don't." Ethan blinked away the sting in his eyes, turned on his heels, and strode toward the bedroom. "I'll get you some clothes."

"Wait, Ethan, I'm—"

Ethan slammed the door and put his back against it. He slid down the cool wood until he plopped on his rear, staring at their messy bed, the book on the nightstand, and a pair of discarded underwear on the floor.

CHAPTER FIVE

After catching his breath in the bedroom for seconds, minutes, an hour, Ethan gathered some of Peter's old clothes, strode into the kitchen, and shoved them at Nico. The selkie, who could, in fact, make rational, smart decisions, said absolutely nothing. Not when Ethan poured himself another cup of tea, nor when he sat with his grimoire at the table, nose buried between the pages. It wasn't until Ethan dressed in denim pants and a button-down flannel and made for the front door that Nico cleared his throat and said, "Where're you going?"

"The pumpkins need pruning," Ethan snapped and stomped into the cold.

The garden didn't really need attending, but he wanted to stretch his legs, work his hands, do something, anything besides share the lighthouse with Nico Locke. So, Ethan sifted soil, snipped browning leaves, harvested a hearty squash, and at high noon, came across a velvety pelt buried with his sweet onions.

The sealskin was buttery beneath his palms, flecked with spots shaped like skipping stones. His stomach hopped as he turned the pelt over, dragging his palm across the fleshy expanse. *What were you thinking?* He glanced at the shallow pit where the pelt had been haphazardly covered by dirt. *Anyone could've found this.* A selkie's pelt carried with it all their fae-born power. Owning the pelt meant owning the beast, and Nico didn't seem like the type who flourished under ownership. Ethan folded the pelt and placed it inside the woven basket, nestling the furry skin amidst bell-shaped squash, fat tomatoes, sprouts, and radishes.

He hadn't been able to think straight. Hadn't culled the toxicity from his mind. *Your husband thinks you'll cheat on him. You're fruitless. Even the selkie knows there's no chance. Peter will leave you.* He polished a magicked tomato on his jeans and lifted the red globe to his mouth, sinking his teeth in. Juice and seeds splattered on his chin. Icy wind chapped his face, tinged with sea-spray. If Nico—a stranger—could see the truth, the hopelessness, then everyone could. Ethan reminded his lungs to expand. He ate slowly, standing past the garden shed with his back to the lighthouse. Inhaling, exhaling. Allowing the sadness to pass.

"Are you eating that like an apple?" Nico asked, hollering over the sea's loud song.

Ethan chewed. "It's a tomato, and I'm eating it like a tomato."

"I'm sorry about before."

"Which part? Asking about my marriage or tormenting me? Surely it's one or the other." He watched Nico appear in his peripheral. Saw the downward curve of his mouth, the slouch to his brow, how his hair glimmered like a penny in the sunlight. "If Peter had heard you, you'd have a broken nose and nowhere to go. You're a guest here." Ethan turned, meeting the selkie's dark eyes. "What happens in my bedroom is none of your business; what happens between me and my husband is none of your business. What we're going through as a couple is certainly none of your business. Is that clear?"

"Ethan—"

"*Is that clear?*"

"Yes," Nico barked. "Got it. *Clear*. Can I speak?"

Ethan gave him a once-over and turned toward the ocean, chomping the rest of his tomato.

"I know a lifestyle remedy. Not a for sure one—no guarantee—but it goes hand in hand with whatever tea you've invested in. That's why I brought it up. I'm not good at *talking*, I know that. I sounded like an asshole—"

"You were an asshole."

"I *am* an asshole. But reducing your stress, staying off caffeine... And I know it sounds odd, but it's a mountainous orange-lemon thing harvested in Nepal, and eating it improves all this..." Nico gestured to his belly. "My people aren't the most fertile, either, you know. Our pregnancies are difficult—volatile even—shifters tend to be that way."

"And what would you know about being pregnant?" Ethan tested.

"Absolutely nothing. I know what sorrow sounds like, though." Nico's voice weakened, gentled even. "I'm not sure what you've done to me, what your magic's done to me. But I don't think I can handle ever hearing you like that again. The fruit helps. I've seen as such. So, let's go get you some."

Ethan darted his tongue across his lips. Tasted vegetal juice and salt and pine.

How had the stars aligned like this? Ethan, who rarely cried, breaking down on the very night a selkie took shelter in the lighthouse. Magic came with a cost. Every time. Every ritual. But he hadn't expected to find a stranger worming past his defenses, and he truly hadn't prepared for Nico Locke to take any interest in his personal life.

Magic made threads, though, and theirs had formed a stubborn knot.

"We're taking a break for a while. But I appreciate the thought." Ethan tossed the tomato top over the edge of the blackened cliff. "You said you could cook. What'll you need for dinner?"

"Do you like chicken?"

"I do."

"Does Peter?"

"He's not picky."

"All right, then. Chicken it is."

Ethan tried not to look at him. Ignored the way his mind clung to *I know what sorrow sounds like* and *what you've done to me.* He nodded, first at the ocean, then at the lighthouse. "Help me put this harvest away, and then we'll hit the market."

Nico swiped his hand through his hair. Long fingers, tense forearms, flexed shoulders—built like something unbreakable. He followed at Ethan's side, matching him step for step, facing forward, hard-eyed and on a tripwire. Ethan thought a single word might set him off. A too-quick movement or sudden loudness. So, he crept along. Stayed silent. Offered a whispery *thank you* when Nico gripped the door above Ethan's head and held it for him.

There was a certain obscurity that came with feeling a person from the inside, getting a glimpse of their heart and knowing nothing about them. Yet that was where they'd landed. Ethan and Nico. Necromancer and necromanced.

"Shouldn't leave this lying around." Ethan ran the pelt through his hand the same way he would a silk scarf or a horse's tail, feeling the smooth, waterproof material skate across his palm. He draped the pelt on the table and upended the rest of the basket into a colander in the sink.

Ferocity happened in stages. First, Nico hardly moved. Didn't blink. Didn't breathe. Just stood in the living room and stared at the pelt. Second, Ethan felt the air shift at his back. Heard the floor wheeze. Noticed the tension ratchet. He hadn't thought it through—not really. Hadn't considered what finding Nico's pelt might mean in the long run. He'd been too consumed with his own thoughts, his own worries, his own shortcomings, and danger hadn't occurred to him. Hadn't settled in him.

But at the *clank* of a tool loosed from the cutlery block and when Nico's reflection appeared in the glass window above the sink, Ethan realized. When he felt a cool, slender blade rest where his Adam's apple should've been. *There.* That was fae ferocity. Desperate, unhinged, and beastly.

Ethan craned his neck, aiming his chin away from the knife, and rested his wet hands on the edge of the counter. The faucet ran lukewarm, dousing the vegetables.

"I'm no one's servant, witch." Nico's voice trembled.

"If I wanted a servant, I'd be wielding your pelt like a weapon, wouldn't I?" Ethan asked.

He knew better than to show fear. Certainly, Nico could smell it on him though. He swallowed against the yelp building in his throat and angled himself backward. His spine met Nico's chest. Hot breath hit the curve of his cheek.

Nico placed his hand on the countertop and caged Ethan against it. "Is your kindness for show? Did you bring me back from the dead to keep me as a pet? Lure me into submission with a hearth, a meal, and—"

"You're incorrigible," Ethan snapped. His pulse raced. He wanted to reach for his phone. Thought he might lash out with his magic, or beg, or whimper. But he'd done his crying last night, and all he had left was bitterness that made him eager for a fight, for something reckless and shortsighted. He seized Nico's wrist, quick as a snakebite, and gripped until his knuckles paled. "I brought you back because I wanted to see if I could. Because I felt sorry for you. Because I felt *life* in you. If I wanted a servant, I would've kept your pelt hidden until Peter came home, knocked you out with a sleeping spell, and you would've woken tomorrow with shackles 'round your ankles." He pushed Nico's wrist. "Drop it. *Now.*"

Nico made an irritated noise. The knife clattered in the sink.

Ethan could've let it go. Could've exhaled and offered forgiveness, but he heard his husband at the forefront of his mind. *If anyone ever has you, be fast.* Remembered his weakness last night and whipped around. *Make it hurt.* Aimed the sole of his foot at Nico's kneecap, forcing the selkie to trip despite his larger stature. *Use your strength first, magic second.* Nico stumbled. Ethan curled his fingers around the selkie's throat, pressing him against the kitchen island as he crashed to his knees. *Don't be timid. Make them believe you.* Ethan breathed heavily, squeezed until Nico's heartbeat kissed the underside of his knuckles. He'd had to fight before. Had to defend himself, take punches, throw blows. He'd been forced to break things—bones, hearts, promises. Had to figure out when and how someone might aim to hurt him because someone would always, *always* want to.

For becoming self-made, for having a womb, for harnessing magic, for being different.

Nico Locke had known his sweetness and his sarcasm, but he would know Ethan's fierceness too.

"Touch me without my permission again, and I'll sell your pelt to the next trader that breaches our bay," Ethan said and forced Nico to look up. He craned toward him, biting the words at Nico's mouth. "And count your blessings, seal, because I have no more patience for your attitude, your misplaced anger, or your fucking suspicion. The next time you cross me, I'll tear the breath from your lungs." He tightened his grip, conjuring just enough magic to make Nico sputter and wheeze. "Have I been heard?"

Nico gritted his teeth. His cheeks were blush-bitten and apple-red, pupils blown into black saucers. "What've you done to me?" he asked, voice hushed and ragged. He didn't struggle. Didn't try to get away or fight back. Instead, he ran his hand along the outside of Ethan's shin—an absent, accidental touch—and pinched his eyebrows together. "What..." He swallowed tightly. "What is this?"

Ethan steeled his surprise. "It's magic. I put a piece of myself inside you." He didn't know if that was the truth. He'd given his blood, yes. Made an offering, yes. But the lilies served a sacrificial purpose, didn't they? His blood was simply the conduit. He watched anger drain from Nico's face, leaving confusion and something else behind. Defeat, maybe. Acceptance. Ethan leaned closer, placing his mouth dangerously close to the selkie's cheek. "Think about how you'll feel if I rip it back out."

Nico stayed eerily still. "Are you going to tell your husband about this?"

"Which part? The knife or your hand?"

He jerked away from Ethan's knee, moving as if he'd been burned. "Either. Both."

Ethan released Nico's throat and stepped back, smoothing the front of his shirt. "If I tell him, he'll throttle you, too, or send you off on your own, and I'm not sure you'll survive either. So, no. Probably not."

"I don't *get* you," Nico said haughtily. "I almost took your hand off; I don't know how to speak to you; I put a knife to your throat. Why bother with me? What am I to you?"

"An asshole with no manners," Ethan mumbled. He wiped the knife with a rag and slid it back into the cutlery block. "What happened with your pelt? You could've buried it a little deeper at least."

"I wasn't thinking straight. Storm knocked the sense out of me."

Ethan raised a brow. "Seems as though you have no sense to lose."

Nico snorted. "Like I asked before, why bother?"

"Whether you like it or not, I want you to live. Maybe this'll be a story you tell your children or an annoyance you never speak of again, but at least you'll be alive."

"That's not an explanation. Why do I matter? I'm no one to you."

"Because life isn't guaranteed, but it *is* precious. I've given you a second chance. Take it, leave it, I don't care what you do with it. But you'll stay alive until you're well enough to leave. After that? Swim into someone else's net if you want. You won't be my problem."

"A problem, then. That's what I am."

"Yes." Ethan pointed to the shoe rack beside the door. "A hot-headed, stubborn, *rude* problem. Now, put your pelt somewhere safe, lace those boots, borrow one of Peter's coats, and don't speak to me for at least an hour."

Nico's mouth shut with a *click*. Like that, staring at Ethan, Nico's rich brown eyes softened to storm-blue. The longer he stayed out of his pelt, the bluer they became.

Ethan tasted fizzy notes of copper and lemon. Leftover magic popped against the roof of his mouth, remnants of what'd gone unused. He swallowed, wincing at the airy, crackling texture, and made for the door.

Thankfully, Nico held his tongue for the minimum require-ment of one hour, but as soon as the pair stepped into Casper's bustling market, he made an uneasy noise. "Do people take kindly to you here?"

"On occasion, yes. Mostly, no. The townsfolk are nice enough—we're neighbors, after all—but they're cautious." Ethan sighed, sidestepping a booth crowded with caged rodents. "Every-one's been a little unnerved since the storm..." He shrugged, then pointed at a slab of thick-cut bacon in an ice bin and nodded to the butcher. "I try not to let it bother me."

The butcher wrapped the bacon in white paper and handed it over. "Anything else, Mr. Vásquez?"

Ethan hadn't taken Peter's last name, but the sentiment still floated around town. Sometimes Peter was Shaw; most of the time Ethan was Vásquez. He turned toward Nico. "You wanted chicken, didn't you?"

Nico nodded. "A whole chicken, if you have it," he said to the butcher.

"Live or defeathered?"

"Defeathered."

The butcher reached into a cooler behind the booth and pulled a pale-skinned bird from the icebox. He wrapped it in plastic, then paper, and tied the package with brown string. He handed the chicken to Nico, and Ethan slipped his card into the chip reader attached to a portable register.

"I should probably find my wallet sometime soon," Nico murmured. His eyebrows pulled together with confused concentration. "I'll pay you back—"

"You probably have a bit of amnesia. It'll pass." Ethan waved his hand dismissively. "Besides, you're our very rude, very broody guest."

Nico huffed. "You're tiny and awful. You know that, right?"

"I do."

After that, Ethan ducked beneath a row of leather bags and made his way into the belly of the market, sheltered by tarps and weatherproof cloth strung between brick buildings. Like most places people came to explore, Casper was buckled together with oddities. The market was strangest of all. It was a town that leaned into rumors, most of which were half-true, and profited off the curiosity tourists and travelers brought to its streets. Faux lilies were, of course, the biggest draw, followed by bags of seeds that would never grow but promised true love, rose petals mixed with bee pollen sold as cures for ailments, and seaweed scented like the finest perfume. Fish skeletons and walrus skulls, beach agates and sun-dried kelp, all worthless trinkets pawned as wonderments. Amidst the peculiarities, traders set up shop, selling luxuries from different places: Chinese silks, Turkish candy, Palestinian scarves, Korean treats—even Nepalese fruits. Ethan tried to ignore the oblong citrus in a painted bowl, but Nico seized his elbow, stopping him in place.

"See." Nico leaned over the shadowy table. "These things. They're the fruit I told you about."

The trader sat in a foldout chair, reading a floppy gossip magazine. She eyed Ethan over the top of her round glasses. "Like an orange but with—" She kissed the air and sucked her teeth. "—salty aftertaste. Lime meets tangerine." She was a plump, crinkled woman with lush black hair and working hands. "Snow plum will bring you abundance."

"May I?" Ethan asked. When she nodded, he picked one up. The snow plum was about the size of a lemon with mottled purplish skin and a short stem flecked with a baby leaf. He brought it to his nose. It smelled sweet and mild. He imagined the flavor was the same. "How much?"

"Fifty," she said without hesitating.

"You're kidding."

"Do I look like I'm kidding?" The trader smiled and dog-eared a page in her magazine, then closed it politely in her lap. "Ask nicely, and I'll consider forty."

"For *fruit*? Thirty," Ethan countered.

"Thirty-five, and I'll give you two, one fresh, one on the verge of turning."

"Turning?"

"It'll need to be eaten within the week. The other will last a month in the refrigerator. If you want abundance, here it is. Wealth. Prosperity. Ripeness." She shot him a knowing glance, shoes to nose, and her smile stretched. "Deal?"

He sighed, annoyed. He hadn't wanted to think about it. *Fertility this, barren that.* Hadn't wanted to let the unease fester. Still, he said, "Fine, deal."

Ethan paid for the fruit and took the small paper bag she handed over.

"Raw," she said. Her mouth opened wide for the word, and she spoke from the back of her throat, hanging onto the bag until he met her eyes. "A little sugar is fine, but no baking, no sautéing. Heat will simmer off the magic."

"And...and what about intent? Do I need to...to focus or—"

"Magic knows," she said and released the bag. "Peel, chew, swallow. The rest will come."

He stepped away from the table, bumping Nico's chest, and righted himself in the narrow walkway between booths and tables. He didn't know what else to say, regretted making the purchase, regretted hugging some silly cosmic fruit—probably another market forgery—against his chest, and regretted putting any stock in Nico's stories. Yet there he was, hurrying through the market with his head down, ignoring Nico saying his name again and again and—

"Ethan," Nico barked and pawed at his hand. "What is it? What's wrong?"

"Nothing," he said and then again, more fully, "nothing. She was a weird lady; that's all. What else do you need for your chicken?"

Nico lifted an eyebrow. "Lemon, rosemary, and cheap beer."

"Cheap beer," Ethan parroted, shaking his head. "I have enough rosemary to last a year. We can get lemon and beer at the grocer; c'mon."

"Do you like potatoes?"

"Everyone likes potatoes."

Nico hopped to keep up. "Okay, do you *have* potatoes?"

"Yes, Nico, I have potatoes."

"What about a vegetable? Carrots? Salad?"

"I can make a salad if you'd like."

"*I* can make it. I just—"

"Yes, Nico, we have the ingredients to make a salad," Ethan said.

An unexpected smile crept to his face. Maybe it was the bag squished against his chest, or the familiarity blooming between him and the hostile selkie that'd washed onto his shore, or the attention Peter had given him this morning. Maybe he was feeling a type of relief he'd never experienced, or maybe the scent of the fruit had calmed his nerves, or maybe he'd needed to give himself another outlet, another way to revisit the idea of creation, parenthood, *life*.

Where hope trembled like an arrow ready to loose, fear stripped away his armor. Left him bare and easy to hurt.

Even so, after everything, Nico Locke made him curious.

"The fruit'll work," Nico assured.

Ethan guided them onto the misty sidewalk and shook his head. "Maybe. Let's not jinx it though."

Again, Nico stopped him. This time, he took Ethan's wrist, circling his pulse in a tender hold. "My pelt is my freedom," he said, swallowing hard. "Most people would take it without thinking twice. Would take me. I know it's not an excuse, but trust doesn't come easy, and you...you disarm me. I'm sorry for before—*I am*—but I need you to understand that I'm trying *very* hard to keep my wits about me. I can't remember...anything, really."

"A bit of memory loss is normal after what you've been through."

"Well, you and your husband make it difficult to stay on guard."

"You're a fool," Ethan said accidentally. He stared at Nico over the slope of his shoulder, studying his pinched mouth and furrowed brow. "Like I've said multiple times, I have no interest in servitude. Trust might not be easy, but if your caution comes with physical threats on my life—"

"That was a mistake."

"One that would've cost you if we hadn't been alone."

Nico licked his lips, heaving a tired sigh.

"My husband is a gentle, good man. Sweet as honey. And I've never been more serious when I tell you he would've killed you with his bare hands if you'd done what you had while he was home. He is gentle," Ethan repeated, saying each word slowly. "He is good. But he's also ruthless and well-acquainted with defending us. He's a man who would bring a seal home and try to save it. He's a man who would cut your throat if you touched me without my permission." He shifted his eyes downward. Nico immediately released his wrist. "He's a man who thinks you're wild and handsome," Ethan added, allowing his mouth to split into a teasing grin. "And I'm sure he doesn't believe you could *ever* be domesticated because of him."

The selkie's cheeks darkened. His mouth made the shape of the word *domesticated*, and he shifted from foot to foot. "You confuse me. You both do."

"I confuse myself." Ethan shrugged toward the store at the end of the block. "Now, c'mon."

Ethan went and Nico followed. They passed the bookstore and Specter Café, and Ethan swiveled toward the window as they passed the herbiary. Inside, Lucia Belle stood with their arms folded. Their customer looked distraught, her face crumbled with sadness or anger—both, perhaps—and she brought her fist down on the counter, startling the shop cat. Lucia caught his gaze through the glass. Their impatient expression morphed to an *ah-hah* as if they'd remembered something important.

Ethan knocked into Nico's shoulder, mumbled an apology, and hurried toward the grocer.

CHAPTER SIX

"What on God's green earth are you doing with that chicken?" Ethan tipped his head, watching Nico crack open a Pabst Blue Ribbon and stuff the can into the belly of the bird.

"You've never had beer-in-the-butt-chicken before?" Nico jerked his head backward and shot Ethan a bewildered look. "Did you really think I'd buy PBR to *drink*?"

"No, I can't say I have, and I didn't take you for a beer snob, so." Ethan shrugged.

The lighthouse was pleasantly warm, kept cozy by a crackling fire and the hot oven. Nico's pelt was neatly folded on the sitting chair beside the hearth, and the kitchen counter was cluttered with ingredients. Peeled potatoes boiled on the stove, and salad fixings were trimmed and chopped on a cutting board. Nico rubbed the chicken with rosemary, parsley, stone-ground mustard, pureed bell pepper, and minced garlic, staring far too intently at the headless bird.

"I'm not a beer snob; I just have taste." Nico narrowed his eyes at the chicken, obscenely skewered on the beer can. "It'll fit in your oven, right?"

"If we adjust the rack, yes."

"Where's your salt and pepper?"

Ethan rounded the kitchen island and opened the cupboard. He swatted Nico's wandering hand, halting him inches from the vial of siren marrow. "Here," he snapped and shoved the saltshaker into his palm, standing on his tiptoes to find the pepper grinder. When Nico turned back to the chicken, Ethan hurriedly pushed the marrow between a bottle of vanilla extract and a sack of powdered sugar. He took out the pepper and set it on the counter. "How long will it take to cook?"

"An hour and a half." Nico looked comical wearing mismatched mittens, one yellow, the other pink. He placed the chicken in the oven and crouched to stare at it, clinging to the steel handle with his nose an inch from the transparent door.

"Oh, good. Well, Peter should be home—"

A key turned in the lock.

Ethan finished his statement with a nod. "—now, I guess. Evening, darling. How was the boat?"

"Wet." Peter uncoiled his scarf, hung it with his coat on the rack, and toed off his boots. "Gulls everywhere; harbor porpoise got chased off by a pod of orca." He paused to sigh, shaking his head. "Damn whales swim into the shallows and scare off our catch."

"It's early for them, isn't it?" Ethan asked.

Peter tipped his head, considering. "Yes and no. They're unpredictable. Autumn, winter, early spring—all fair game."

"Nasty behemoths," Nico said. He took off the mittens and scanned the counter, then the pantry. "Do you two drink...? I haven't seen anything other than beer and wine, which is fine, but I—"

"Top shelf," Ethan and Peter said in unison.

Peter kissed Ethan's temple as he walked by, slipping past Nico to search the pantry. He pulled an amber bottle from the shelf and tipped the label toward him. "Not the best, but it'll keep you warm," he said, gesturing to his belly. "How do you take your liquor?"

"However you decide to pour it," Nico said.

Ethan noticed how Nico braved glances at Peter. How his gaze lingered, eyes tracking each step Peter took through the kitchen. There was an air of curiosity, as if Nico had decided to *try* for acceptance. As if he'd convinced himself to trust, to be interested, to wonder. Nico raked his fingers through his hair. Peter squeezed lemon juice into three short glasses.

"Whiskey sour it is," Peter said. He glanced at Ethan. "You too?"

Ethan nodded. "Sure. Do we need an orange?"

"Some type of fruit, yes."

Nico lifted a brow. "Ethan picked up a couple snow plums at the market today. They'd work, right?"

"Snow plums?" Peter asked.

"Nepalese fruit. Thought we'd try something new." Ethan cleared his throat and shot Nico a deadly glance. *Do not.* "We have oranges though. Take your pick."

"Surprise me," Peter said.

This time, Nico tipped his head, saddling Ethan with a look that said *go on.*

Ethan wanted to ignore him, but his hand drifted toward the paper bag on the table. He reached inside, palming a snow plum. Unlike the marrow buried in their spice cupboard, the fruit wasn't euphoric and wouldn't change their behavior. *Right...?* It was fruit—*just a fruit*—and a peel-coil wouldn't hurt. He sank his thumbnail into the meaty skin and pulled, exposing pale, white citrus beneath. It perfumed the air, that odd, lemony stink, and Ethan couldn't suppress the anxious flutter in his chest. Hope brewed over a low flame flickering in his gut. Anticipation throbbed in his teeth and toes and stomach. He handed the peel to Peter and brought a naked slice to his mouth, nibbling on the snow plum. Sweetness burst on his tongue, followed by smoke, tang, and then a sourness that puckered his lips. He ate one slice, then another, and held the fruit out to Peter.

"Try it," Ethan said.

Peter leaned forward and took a slice with his teeth, nipping Ethan's fingertips. "Weird," he said while he chewed and furrowed his brow. "Reminds me of a funny grape. Like, a sour one you get on New Year's for a bad month, you know?"

"What?" Nico asked, then mumbled, "Thank you," under his breath as Peter handed him a drink.

"Las doce uvas de la suerte?" Peter frowned, sighing patiently. "Bad luck not to eat grapes on New Year's Eve," he said, like a parent would to a child. "You eat one every minute for the first twelve minutes of the new year. Each grape represents a month. The grapes that're sour or squishy represent bad months; the sweet ones represent good months. It's tradition."

Nico nodded slowly. "I've never done the grape thing. We dress meals for spirits though. Hang their pelts on the back of empty chairs and eat with them until midnight. Clearing plates set for the dead before morning brings bad fortune—like ruining an al-tar—so, we all ask our ancestors if we can take bites. The kids do at least. My dad used to pretend to hear our grandfather. He'd tell us grandpa only shared his cabbage." He sipped his drink. "This is good, thank you."

Peter gave a single, slow nod. "How's your side?"

"A little sore."

"Let's take a look," he said and rolled his sleeves to his elbows.

Ethan paused midchew of the snow plum. He watched Nico's pupils expand, his eyes dart across Peter's forearms, and caught the distinct bob in his throat as he swallowed. "I can do it myself. I'm sure I'm—"

"Don't be foolish," Peter said. He pushed his glasses up and looked at Ethan over his shoulder. "Get more bandages, will you?"

Ethan took a long pull from his drink, set the glass on the table, and went to retrieve the bandages from the washroom. He stepped back into the kitchen just as Nico tugged off his shirt and stared at the pinkish spot bleeding through the gauze wrapped around his chest. Their scuffle earlier must've strained the wound.

"I'll get the salve too," Ethan said. "How's your pain level, Nico?"

"It still itches." Nico shrugged. "And it's sore, but not bad. Feels better than yesterday."

Peter eased the last of the bandage away. "It's not as red which means your chances of infection are going down. Tell me where it starts to hurt." He walked two fingers across Nico's rib cage, and just shy of the wound, Nico flinched. "There, then?"

Nico nodded.

"Let me," Ethan said and eased into the space next to Peter.

There they were, Peter and Ethan side by side, crowded into Nico's space, tending to his wounds. Nico blushed furiously, and Ethan's mouth curved upward.

Peter mumbled, "Careful," when Ethan smeared the ointment onto Nico's wound, as gentle and worrisome as he always was.

They weren't comfortable, but the trio was aware of one another. Aware and at peace with the unknown. Somewhere, a sliver of Ethan stirred inside Nico, and somewhere, a bit of Ethan stirred inside Peter, too, and somehow, Ethan felt grounded. Safe. He remembered Nico's strained voice—*what've you done to me*—and thought he might've felt their shared magic pulse and tremble, might've felt the thread between them go taut. When Ethan lifted his face, Nico's eyes were lidded, his lips parted.

"Are you all right?" Ethan asked.

The selkie nodded. "I should check the chicken."

"Let's get you patched up first." Peter rested his palm on Ethan's tailbone, coaxing him sideways, and then went to work rewrapping Nico's chest. Nico allowed it. Stayed perfectly still, flicking his attention between Ethan and Peter, necromancer and captain, magician and seaman.

"Ethan tells me you're quite a fisherman," Nico said.

Peter snorted, grinning sheepishly. "I caught you, didn't I?"

At that, Nico's blush worsened, and Ethan drained the rest of his whiskey.

"Be nice, Peter," Ethan said.

"Oh, I'm joking." Peter clipped the bandages into place and righted himself. "But, yeah, I guess I have a good sense of the tide. What about you, did you study a trade?"

"I can hunt."

"I don't doubt that."

Ethan cleared his throat. "I should adjust the lamp timer," he blurted, pointing at the ceiling. The lamp was probably fine, but he needed a moment alone. Time to think. To understand what exactly was going on between the three of them. "I'll be right back."

Nico narrowed his eyes. Peter sat at the table, fingering the snow plum peel soaking in his glass. Neither moved to stop him when Ethan darted toward the spiral staircase and climbed the steps. He steadied his breathing as he followed the stairs up and up and *up* until he unlatched an overhead door and hoisted into the lamp room.

Glass panels stretched from floor to ceiling, curving outward toward the sky and sea. The cylindrical lamp glowed, and droplets streaked the windows. Ethan kicked out his legs, shook away the restlessness growing in his limbs, and wrung his hands. He thought of the siren marrow, the snow plum, the selkie pelt folded on his recliner. Thought of Peter's distrust when Nico had first walked into the lighthouse, and the warmth he'd extended downstairs. How his husband spoke to Nico kindly, playfully. How Nico looked at Peter hungrily, timidly. He thought of Nico kneeling before him, feathering his mouth across Nico's chin, finding himself feverish at the creeping thought that Nico might *want* him.

Now, he found himself completely apprehended by the thought that Peter might want Nico too. That they all might want one another.

"Absolutely the fuck not," Ethan mumbled. He rested his forehead on the cold glass and stared at the waves.

Peter wasn't fickle. He was steadfast, devoted, and sturdy. He wasn't the type to change his opinion of something or some*one* overnight. This shift in behavior, this invitation for flirtation reminded Ethan of years ago, of prowling the local pub, making out behind the church, commenting on who they found appealing in town when they both damn well knew they only had eyes for each other.

What if the awkward dance of attraction and irritation between Ethan and Nico had leaked into his marriage? Ethan swallowed thickly. What if he'd made a terrible mistake telling Peter about his insecurities, raising a selkie from the dead, and opening their home to a stranger? Grasping at feeble hope shaped like bone marrow and exotic fruit? Letting his eyes wander to a man who was *not* his husband?

"Honey, dinner's almost ready," Peter called.

Ethan chewed his bottom lip. He felt dirty, caked in infidelity he hadn't committed. "I'll be right down!"

Just as he'd thought, the lamp didn't need adjusting, but he checked the timer anyway. He took a polishing cloth to the place his forehead had smudged the window and convinced his heart to slow. Maybe he'd misread the entire situation. Maybe it was Ethan who *wanted*, and neither of the men downstairs had anything to do with his loneliness, his curiosity, his wonderment. He truly hated being this way—wanting everything and nothing, reaching for the magic he'd purposefully hidden inside another person, yearning for a child and knowing he would probably never have one. Fear filled him like an old wound, still cracked and leaking, shaped like a storm.

That's what's wrong with me. I'm utterly unhinged.

Maybe it was true; maybe it wasn't.

Either way, he told his desire to behave, relatched the door, and descended the staircase.

The hearth crackled, and wax puddled in the candelabra's iron palms. Nico stood with his hip propped against the kitchen island, smiling as Peter rattled on about the day's crab catch. The pair was framed by herb bundles strung above the sink, firelight glinting off the copper kitchenware, their messy countertops riddled with spices, wooden tasting spoons, and half-diced salad ingredients. Everything felt normal in a way Ethan hadn't expected. Deliriously domestic. Softened by whiskey and close quarters.

"Did you mash the potatoes?" Ethan asked.

Nico blinked away from Peter and nodded. "The chicken's 'bout ready. I've almost got the salad done. Just needs cheese and croutons."

"We've still got a bit of peppered goat cheese left, don't we? That'd be nice with the spinach," Peter said.

Ethan smiled. *Go with it. Make the best of this.* "Yeah, it would. Let's do that, then."

While Peter got the cheese out of the fridge, Nico pulled the hot chicken from the oven. The lighthouse reeked of rosemary, thyme, butter, and cooked bird, and the dishes clanked when Ethan set the table. Once the potatoes were mashed and the chicken was cut, they sat and dressed their plates. Peter fixed them each another cocktail, and Ethan insisted on crostini instead of croutons.

That night, before he touched his food, Nico bowed his head and mouthed the words to a silent prayer. The selkie kissed the center of his palm and lifted his face, clearing his throat the moment Ethan met his gaze.

"Let's eat," Nico said.

"Thank you for cooking." Peter stabbed a thick piece of chicken and brought the whole thing to his mouth. "Where'd you learn how to move around the kitchen like that?"

"My mother taught me."

"I didn't know you were a man of faith," Ethan said. He kept his attention on his food, slicing chicken breast, drizzling pumpkin vinaigrette over his salad. He hadn't meant to ask about religion at the dinner table. *How crass.* "Sorry, that was—"

"Raised Catholic," Nico said, shrugging. He stuffed his mouth, chewed, swallowed. "I wouldn't call myself a man of faith, but I pray here and there. I go to mass on Christmas and Easter. I take communion when I can. It's a ritualistic part of my life, I guess." He paused, salting his potatoes. "A comfort."

"I have a lot of religious family." Peter sipped his drink and shot Ethan a narrow-eyed glance. "I'm not close with many of them, but..." He tipped his head, mulling. "Sometimes, they reach out, persuade me to go to church. They worry, you know. Estoy con un brujo."

"Oh, so it's *my* fault you're a heretic," Ethan teased.

"Gossip travels far and fast. My sister heard about Katia, told our mother; Mama told Abuela. They assumed, I'm sure."

Nico nodded. "Assumed you turned away from God?"

"Being magicked back to life by the town alchemist tends to have that effect, yes." Peter adjusted his glasses, offering a crooked smile. "Marrying him gave my family a heart attack to begin with. They thought I'd been hexed." He stroked Ethan's wrist.

"Still a possibility." Ethan turned his hand over, allowing Peter to touch his palm. He waved his fork between Peter and Nico. "I could have you both under a spell, truthfully."

"Is that right?" Peter scoffed. He jutted his chin toward Nico. "How 'bout you, bein' fae-blooded and all? Would it even be possible for my husband to put *you* under a spell?"

"If you'd asked me that two days ago, I would've said no," Nico admitted.

Ethan blushed. "And now?"

Nico busied himself with his dinner, ignoring the question until Ethan cleared his throat. Nico shifted his jaw. "I'd say you've enchanted me." He swallowed a mouthful of whiskey. "I'd call you both wizards. Claim you've spelled me, somehow."

"*Wizards*," Peter exclaimed, barking through a laugh. His wide, white grin was contagious.

Ethan tried not to laugh, but he couldn't temper his smile. "Wizardry, then. I guess that's what we'll tell the town." He clanked his glass against Peter's, chuckling. "We've accidentally wrangled ourselves a selkie who can cook and *spelled* him into liking us."

Peter snorted, cheeks reddened from liquor and laughter. "Good for us, darling. Praise be."

A reluctant smile curved Nico's mouth. His shoulders loosened, and he relaxed in his seat, raising a tapered brow. "You think you've wrangled me?"

"Haven't we?" Ethan asked, and at the same time, Peter nodded and said, "Looks that way."

Ethan met Nico's gaze. His light eyes glinted gold in the candlelight, more animal than man, and Ethan remembered earlier that day, the knife pressed to his throat, then knocking Nico to the floor and sending magic pulsing through the air. Tension thickened, constricted unbearably, and left him hungry for answers to questions he was afraid to ask, curious about a man who'd crashed into their life—into his marriage.

The conversation ebbed, and they went back to their dinner, scooping potatoes, nibbling chicken, stuffing their mouths with spinach and bread. Once they'd finished, Nico settled atop a quilt in front of the hearth, and Peter sat in the recliner. Ethan plopped on the floor between Peter's calves, leaning against the leather chair. His eyes curtained as the fire popped. Peter traced the shell of his ear and played absently with his hair, and flames sent shadows across Nico's long, pretty features.

"How'd you get me here?" Nico asked, his brows furrowed, and he turned to face them, glancing from Ethan to Peter. "I'm not dainty in either skin."

"I rolled you here on a fishery palette. I tried to carry you—almost succeeded—but hauling you uphill wasn't in the cards," Peter said. "I put a towel over your face like they do in those veterinarian shows though."

Nico laughed in his throat. "What'd your crew think?"

"That I'd lost my mind."

"What'd you think?" Nico asked, flicking his gaze to Ethan.

Ethan sipped his drink. Liquor burned his throat. "I thought you were a lot more than a sad, lifeless seal, and I was right. My husband bringing you home was no surprise though. You should see him in spring, making nurseries for abandoned birds and putting leftovers out for raccoons."

"I'm shocked you don't have a dog," Nico said. "Or a cat. A pet of some sort."

"Our focus has been elsewhere." Peter ran his finger along Ethan's jaw. "A dog might be nice though. Bring some pawprints to the lighthouse. What do you think?"

Ethan nodded—not yes, not no—but acknowledgement. "Something of our own," he murmured before realizing he'd spoken aloud. He heaved a sigh to try to distract from his solemn statement. "Is your aunt aware that you're here?" he asked Nico. He finished the rest of his drink. His mind was delightfully slow, thoughts moving like molasses. "Did you have a phone or, I don't know, belongings anywhere?"

Nico blinked, taken aback. He tilted his head and searched the floor, the fire, then the ceiling. "Yeah," he said, laughing softly. "Yeah, I do. I hadn't thought about...any of that, actually. Except my wallet, but... But I was staying at the Casper Inn. I'm sure they've... Well, I'm sure they've thrown my shit out by now—"

"Like I said at the market, a little post-spell amnesia isn't uncommon. Especially postmortem," Ethan assured.

"I forgot my middle names for a while after," Peter said. "Took a minute to get those back."

Nico nodded. He looked adorably confused, cheeks reddened by whiskey, lips pursed, eyes squinted.

"We can call the inn if you want." Ethan fished his phone out of his pocket. "Or you can call. How long was your reservation for?"

"I was supposed to check out on November seventh. What's the date?" Nico asked, laughing again. He swiped his hand through his hair, leaning backward to brace on his palm.

"It's only the sixth." Ethan held out his phone. "Go on. Call."

Nico took the phone and made for the front door.

Peter yawned and stretched. His ankles cracked. "I should clean the kitchen and get to bed," he said, curling his knees inward to squeeze Ethan's upper arms. "Come with me?"

Ethan watched a shadow cross the bottom of the door. He could've slept; he could've stayed awake. Could've journaled or taken a bath, could've fallen asleep in the recliner or curled up next to the fire. But Peter's thumb grazed the place where Ethan's neck hinged, throat to jaw, and he knew the intention in a touch like that. The question. He pushed to his feet and got to work clearing the table, leaning into Peter's hands drifting across his waist as they moved around the kitchen, filling containers with leftover potatoes and washing dishes in soapy water.

"He's calmed down a bit," Peter said.

Ethan nodded. "You have too."

"Have I?" Heat sparked, popping like a wick.

He shot Peter a questioning look. "Correct me if I'm wrong, but from where I'm standing, yes."

Nico opened the door just as Ethan was toweling his hands.

"I can pick up my things tomorrow." Nico gripped his wrist, hands clutched nervously at his beltline. "The manager said they'd hold my room too. Extend my stay if I need a soft place to land while I recoup."

"Is that what you'd like to do, then?" Peter asked. He took off his glasses and cleaned them with his shirt. He clucked his tongue, staring at Nico with fond, curious eyes. "Or would you rather stay here?"

Ethan parted his lips, struggling with excuses. *I'll need to check your bandages* and *it's best you're close while you heal* and *don't go* and *not yet.*

"I'd prefer to stay here until I can swim again. If you'll have me—or, I mean—if that's all right." Nico flashed a shy smile. "You've already wrangled me, so."

"True." Peter gave a curt nod and disappeared into the bedroom, tossing a casual, "See you in the morning," over his shoulder as he went.

Ethan met Nico's eyes. They stayed like that, watching each other until a dresser drawer noisily opened and closed.

"Pleasant dreams, Nico," Ethan said and eased the bedroom door halfway closed, waiting.

Nico turned toward the hearth. "Good night."

Rusted hinges wheezed and creaked, and Ethan shut the bedroom door with a faint *click*, memorizing the shape of Nico bathed in firelight, standing in the middle of the lighthouse.

CHAPTER SEVEN

The night had gone unexpectedly.

Once Ethan had locked their bedroom, Peter had pawed at him, manhandling him against the wall, the closet door, the dresser. Ethan hadn't anticipated that—Peter's lips scorching a path down his throat, being hoisted onto the dresser and fiercely kissed. He'd clutched to Peter, whimpered and spread his legs, overcome with suddenness, aggression, *heat*.

"What's gotten into you?" Ethan had tried and failed to calm his thundering heart. "First you hate him, and then you're jealous of him. Tonight, you're his best fuckin' pal, and now you're acting like a damn lion. I'm not a gazelle, Peter. You don't have to mark your territory."

Peter tugged him, turned him, and forced his palms against the top of the dresser. He yanked impatiently at his pants. "Tell me to stop, then," he purred, nuzzling Ethan's nape.

"He has ears like a dog—he'll hear us," Ethan snapped, whispering furiously. He quivered, pants and underwear bunched at his ankles, hopelessly wet and aching to be touched. He'd been horribly, painfully embarrassed when Peter reached between his legs and grazed his slit, and he'd hardly contained a pitiful whine.

"Don't you *want* him to hear us?" Peter teased, his voice a harsh rasp against Ethan's ear. "I think you do. You want him to hear everything, querido. Want him to imagine what's goin' on in here—want to make him sweat. Tell me I'm lying."

"I... It's... Fuck, are you punishing me? Is this a test?" Ethan whimpered, bracing on the furniture as the rake of a zipper came and went.

"I'm indulging us," Peter said, breathing hard, grip bruise-tight on Ethan's hips. "I see the way you look at him."

"I see the way *you* look at him," Ethan snapped back. Stubble scraped his neck, and Peter seized his chin, pulling him into another messy kiss.

"Then we've come to an understanding, no?"

By the time Ethan had opened his mouth to speak, Peter had filled him on a single, fluid thrust. Every thought emptied. He grasped at the frayed edges of something impossible—that Peter wanted Nico, that Peter wanted *him* to want Nico—and endured the fast, relentless sex he'd silently begged for. The rough hold on his body, the sound of their skin meeting, the soft, pathetic sounds he couldn't keep at bay. Ethan hadn't prepared for that. For Peter Vásquez to become ravenous, for their shared secrecy to come alive inside their bedroom, put on display and welcomed. Yes, he wanted Nico. Of course, he wanted Nico. They both did. The thought crashed around inside him.

"I do," Ethan confessed, whispering in the dark. "I want him to hear us."

They'd fucked like that, with Ethan bent over the dresser, half-clothed and trembling, knowing Nico could hear his small cries, his shaken whimpers, his gasps and wobbly pleas. The whiskey had dulled his inhibitions, made him eager and messy and malleable. When Peter plunged two fingers past his lips, he gagged and moaned, and when his husband forced his jaw to slacken, his mouth to stay open, allowing those rough, throaty noises to escape, Ethan gushed around his cock. *Loved* it. Clenched and spasmed and came because of it.

In the moments after, shame churned in Ethan's gut. After Peter cleaned him with a towel from the hamper, kissed him sweetly, and guided him to bed, he'd tossed and turned, thinking of Nico in the living quarters, listening.

In the morning, Peter got ready for work. He pecked Ethan on the lips, brushed his cheek with calloused knuckles, and said, "I love you."

"I love you too." What else was there to say? It was an unchallenged truth, even then, even after last night. "Are we okay, Peter? Don't *indulge* me; tell me the truth. Are we?"

Peter's eyes softened in the new morning light. "We do this together, or we don't do it at all. Sí?"

"What is 'this'?" he asked, exasperated.

"Opening our marriage," Peter said and kissed his forehead. "It happens together, or it doesn't happen."

Ethan didn't know what to say. He blew out a breath, searching Peter's face.

"Right?" Peter asked.

"Right, yes," Ethan blurted, flabbergasted. "Of course."

Peter pinched his chin and slipped out of their bedroom. "Morning, patrón," he said to Nico, then slung on his coat and shut the front door quietly behind him.

What...? Ethan sat cross-legged on their bed and bundled the sleeves of his nightshirt into his palms. The blue hour lit the tower varying shades of navy, seafoam, and black. The sound of the sink running broke the quiet. Kettle bottom met iron on the stovetop, and Nico's socked feet shuffled over the tile. Ethan's mind was liquor-whipped and cottony, clinging to sleep the same way mist clung to Casper. He massaged his temples. Rallying bravery, he stepped into a pair of sweats and tightened the drawstring around his waist.

Peter's voice rang through him. *Opening our marriage.* Each word landed like a mule kick to Ethan's chest. *Opening our marriage.* As if they'd locked something away when they'd taken their vows. *Opening our marriage.* Like Nico had blown open an urge they'd ignored for a decade. *Opening our marriage.* They'd never talked about it, never been given an opportunity to entertain the idea.

Forty-eight hours with a handsome stranger had changed *everything.*

Ethan tried to calm the anxious knot in his stomach, fought against the heat filling his cheeks, and stepped into the living quarters.

Nico tipped the steaming kettle over a mug. "Did you rest well?"

"Yes," he lied, nodding. "And you?"

Nico lifted a brow. "Had trouble falling asleep." He gave a coy snort. "You didn't happen to hear an overzealous couple going at it like porn stars, did you? I could've sworn—"

"Listen, I..." Ethan set his teeth hard. Embarrassment flared. Caused his head to spin. He exhaled sharply, staring at the counter and then the ground. "I wasn't clearheaded last night, and I'm sorry. I don't...I don't know what's going on with me, or Peter—with *us*—but that was rude and—"

Nico placed a bent knuckle beneath Ethan's chin and lifted his face. "What happens in your bedroom is none of my business," Nico murmured, pressing his thumb to Ethan's bottom lip. "What happens between you and your husband is none of my business, and what you're going through as a couple is *certainly* none of my business." The very same words Ethan had used, the same rhythm, the same cadence. Nico snarled a smile, his breath coasting Ethan's slack mouth. "*Right?*"

Heat pooled in Ethan's groin. He snapped his teeth around Nico's thumb, a fast, petty bite. Nico hissed and jerked away, snaring him in a fierce glare.

"You're a menace," Ethan hissed.

"And you're a coward."

"How *dare* you—"

It was then that Nico kissed him.

The selkie moved with purpose, cupped Ethan's jaw, and brought their mouths together. Ethan warmed under the weight of his lips. Arched into him like the tide, pulled inward, gravitating toward something solid and constant and new. *Harder*, he thought, and tipped his head. Nico's teeth knocked his own. Then he heard Peter's voice again—*it happens together, or it doesn't happen*—and opened his eyes.

He eased away, shivering at the sound of their lips parting. Nico watched him carefully, pupils blown, eyes half-curtained, and closed the space between them, kissing him again. This time, Ethan welcomed the warm, wet pass of Nico's tongue behind his teeth before he set his palms on Nico's chest and pushed. Nico pulled away, and Ethan pushed him again, putting an arm's length between them. He swallowed, feverish, shaken, and confused. His fingers twitched, extended toward Nico, keeping a wild thing at bay.

"Not without my husband," Ethan rasped. Magic coursed through him, tilting the air, causing everything to thicken and buzz. "We can't do this without Peter."

Strange, kissing someone who wasn't the person he'd kissed as a teen, as a young man, as who he was at twenty-nine. Nico tasted like black tea and kelp, kissed like someone who had kissed many different mouths, looked at him with wide, dangerous eyes. He gave a tense nod.

"You know your way to the inn, don't you?" Ethan asked, hand still outstretched.

Again, Nico nodded. His expression fractured. "If you want me to go, I'll go. I can stay there—"

"I just meant to get your things. Don't be dramatic." Ethan sighed, pushing his hand through his hair. His teeth weren't clean. He needed to shower—God, he *really* needed to shower—and talk to his sweet, stupid, tolerant husband, and clear his head. "I need to run a few errands. Can you manage a visit to the inn by yourself? I'll only be an hour or two."

"Yeah, I'll be fine." Nico's throat flexed. He looked handsome and eerie in the silver light coming through the window, freckled and sharp with his fae features and webbed hands. He inhaled deeply and exhaled like a sad dog, dragging his gaze from Ethan's feet to his face. "You're not a coward," he said, defeated. "You're kind and smart and good, and you scare me. That's all."

"Well, I stand by what I said—you *are* a menace," Ethan said, half teasing. He put more distance between them. Because he wanted to be held. Because he wanted to kiss Nico Locke again.

Most importantly because he wanted to kiss his husband. "I'll leave the spare key on the table."

Ethan stepped over the unrolled cot on the way to the bedroom. His heart was a runaway, going and going, his palms sweat-slicked. He curled his fingers into fists. Everything inside him pulled excruciatingly tight. *What am I doing?* Magic thrummed and jittered, and his anxiety morphed into nausea.

"Don't do that to me again," Nico blurted.

Ethan halted in the doorway.

"Please," Nico added quietly, then cleared his throat. "Don't."

He glanced over his shoulder. "Don't do what?"

"C'mon, you know exactly what. You wanted me to hear you? I abso-fucking-lutely heard you. Fine, good. Whatever. But if this is a game, and you're playing with me to make your husband jealous—"

"You think last night was my idea?" Ethan laughed. Anger swelled. Pride and impatience did too. His mouth squirmed into a mean smile. He wanted to make his way back to Nico. Strike him with the back of his hand. Bite his throat. Ride him on the kitchen floor. Keeping his feet firmly planted was a practice in self-control. "Peter orchestrated that little show. For you, for me—for all of us. So, if you think you're a plaything, then go." He shrugged toward the entryway. "But don't insult me with your juvenile self-importance. I'm not toying with you, and you don't have the power to come between me and my husband. Have I been heard?"

Nico's jaw flexed. His stony eyes hardened, and he spoke through set teeth. "Yes, Ethan. I've heard you."

"Good," Ethan said and slammed the washroom door behind him.

C asper was busier than normal. People hurried to and from the grocer and bustled around the market, carrying baskets filled with canned goods, linens, and loaves. Ethan pulled his scarf tighter and waved to Miranda Park as he made for the docks.

"Rumor has it that you and Peter have a houseguest," Miranda called. She adjusted the overfilled paper bag in her arms and flashed a grin.

"Rumors are always a little true," Ethan said. He walked backward, watching her plod toward the staircase attached to the crowded café. "I'll call 'bout dinner soon. We'll bake a pie, plan a reading, yeah?"

"You have my number; you know you're always welcome." She waved clumsily, lifting two fingers from the bottom of the bag. "Bring your guest too. I've heard he's a looker!"

Of course. Ethan forced a smile, but before he could turn around, Miranda halted in place.

"Oh! Ethan! Before you go—Lucia was looking for you, I think. You know them? The new shopkeep at the herbiary?"

"Is that right?"

"They have a needy client," Miranda said, cringing. "Figured I'd clue you in."

"*Wonderful.*" Three syllables gusted out on a tired breath. "Thank you. I appreciate the heads-up."

"'Course, dear. I'm holdin' you to that pie!"

"I know, I know. Soon," Ethan hollered. He spun on his heels and shuffled toward the docks.

Miranda had been in Ethan's life since they were children, growing like weeds rooted deep beneath Casper's cobblestone streets. She'd officiated his wedding; he'd practiced simple spells with her. They cooked together in winter; browsed the market, elbows linked, in spring. Loved each other simply, as old companions often did. They shared a lasting friendship he was grateful for. She knew his fear of the sea. Sensed how the unhealed bit of him leftover from Hurricane Katia worsened and festered. Even so, he'd never told her about his waning hope for a child. Not aloud, at least. Never hinted at his heartsickness, though he felt her attentive, tender eyes on it, watching carefully, respecting his boundaries.

Yet Nico, this stranger, this comet the sea had coughed out, had somehow peeked at Ethan's most private worries. Ethan stuffed his hands into the pockets of his wool coat and blinked away thoughts of the selkie. Kissing him; being kissed by him.

The Oyster bobbed against the dock, chunky and scaled with black barnacles. Across from the boat, the dockworkers unloaded the morning haul, transferring giant crabs and lobsters into tubs and tossing red-bellied snapper into ice bins. Peter worked alongside his men, dressed in a windbreaker and a black beanie, laughing as he lifted a crate and stacked it carefully in front of a delivery rig. When he saw Ethan, he paused, brow furrowed, and brushed salty droplets from the front of his jacket.

"What're you doin' here?" Peter asked and tipped his head. He curled his gloved fingers around Ethan's palm. "Everything okay?"

"Yeah, everything's fine. Do you have a minute? Or can you take a quick lunch?"

Peter nodded, turning to holler over his shoulder. "Unload the haul and weigh out the snapper, all right? I'll be back."

His crewmates were a jubilant bunch, shouting, "Aye, cap," and offering friendly greetings to Ethan while they continued the day's work.

Peter tugged at his gloves with his teeth, plucking his fingers free, and clasped Ethan's hand. "Sally's serving chowder today. Unless you'd like to walk or—"

"No, no, let's sit down." Ethan steered them toward the craggy pub situated on the corner where the belly of the town met the docks.

The Golden Clam was Casper's only dive bar. Light from dim lamps illuminated the narrow building, built with red brick and saddled with a stained bar. High-top tables lined the wall, and toward the back of the building, near the kitchen and toilets, four upholstered booths sat unoccupied beneath framed black-and-white photographs of Casper landmarks. As always, Peter chose the booth topped with a photo of the lighthouse—*their* lighthouse—and slid into the seat across from Ethan.

Ethan fiddled with his hands on the tabletop and chewed on the inside of his cheek. Peter watched him expectantly, swiping his beanie off.

"Opening our marriage." Ethan sounded out each word. He swallowed around the lump in his throat and blinked, trying to find a clear path through the conversation. A way to start. A solid direction. "You..." Another breath, another pause. "That's something you want...?"

Peter stayed entirely too still for entirely too long. His mouth was gently set, stubbled jaw relaxed, earthy eyes set on Ethan. He took a deep breath. Didn't nod, didn't shake his head. "It's not something I'm opposed to," he said finally. "If we hadn't met him, maybe not. But we did. And meeting him changed things—"

"Meeting him doesn't have to change anything," Ethan said, deadly serious.

"Ethan, c'mon. Be honest with me."

He rolled his teeth across his bottom lip. Guilt weighed like an anchor in his gut. "He kissed me this morning. I...I kissed him—*we* kissed."

At that, Peter Vásquez stiffened. His shoulders went rigid, and his mouth slackened, but the anger that appeared was gone in an instant, wiped clean and replaced with stoicism. He stayed silent. Blinked and breathed and folded his hands tightly atop the table.

"Talk to me," Ethan whispered. "Tell me where we go from here. I'll make him leave. I'll never speak to him again. I'll—"

"Do you love me?"

Something hot and jagged pricked his throat, thickening his voice. "Of course, I love you. Jesus, Peter. I've loved you for as long as I can remember. I'll *always* love you. I just—"

"Then what're you worried about?"

"Hurting you," Ethan snapped. He sniffled. "Ruining us."

When Peter opened his mouth to speak, Sally Turner appeared beside their booth, notepad in hand, wearing a friendly grin.

"Good to see you, Captain Vásquez. And you, too, Ethan. What can I get you today, hmm?"

Ethan smiled tightly, hoping his eyes didn't look as glassy as they felt. "Tea and chowder, please."

"Same, Sally. Thank you," Peter said.

Sally nodded and circled the bar where she punched their orders into an old computer.

Slowly, Peter reached across the table and covered Ethan's hands with his own. "Mi amor, look at me," Peter said. Ethan pressed his lips together and lifted his eyes. "Your love for me and my love for you aren't weakened by our connection with someone else. Nico fell into our lives and I...I don't know how to feel about it, okay? I don't. But I know you see something in him, and I know I want to understand him, and I know we trust each other enough to explore whatever this is."

Relief battled with the confusion ratcheting inside Ethan. He searched his husband's face—ocean-chapped, ruddy, beautiful—and offered a thoughtful nod. "I don't want you to think this has anything to do with...with *us* though. It doesn't. What's happened with Nico, how I feel about Nico, none of it has anything to do with how I feel about you, or us, or our family. I need you to know that."

"I know." Peter squeezed his hands. "I need you to know that I'm okay with this, whatever it is, as long as we're in it together."

"Yes, yeah, of...of course. I told Nico the same thing this morning. I just... What're we doing, Peter? How do we even navigate this?"

"Did you think of me when you were with him?"

Ethan blushed terribly. He cleared his throat, unlinking their hands as Sally set two steaming bowls of chowder on the table, accompanied by thick-sliced bread and their teas. Once she'd left, he nodded. "It wasn't planned. He... We were talking, he kissed me, I kissed him back, then I stopped it."

"Because you thought of me?" Peter asked calmly.

"Because I won't do anything with him without *you*."

"Then that's how we do this," he said, spooning chowder into his mouth. Peter's boot tapped Ethan's ankle under the table. "We keep loving each other; we keep trusting each other. People do it all the time, darling. That's the thing with love—there's enough to spare. And if it isn't love, if this experience with Nico is physical, period, and we're a pit stop in his life, then... Well, then we enjoy it together."

Ethan stirred his chowder, nodding. His heart felt too big in his chest, weighty and full behind his binder. Of course, this was his husband. Kind and generous and open. Ethan Shaw was lucky. God, he was *so* lucky.

"He's..." Peter adjusted his glasses, a nervous tic. His face reddened. "He's quite beautiful, isn't he?"

"Yeah, he is. I'm sure he knows that though."

Peter snorted. "Seems as much."

"You're fond of him, then? This isn't you reacting to my fondness?"

"I wasn't fond of him—he's a dick—but I watched you two together, and I noticed him noticing me. His attention is difficult to miss."

"He *is* a dick, but he's sweet too. Sometimes. Rarely."

"Noted." Peter smiled.

Ethan dunked his bread into the chowder. "So, you're not angry?"

"That he kissed you?" Peter scooped more chowder into his mouth. Chewed. Swallowed. "Angry isn't the right word. I'm...I'm unused to the idea of someone else kissing you. That's all."

"And you're certain you won't make an attempt on his life if he kisses me in front of you?"

Peter smirked, cheeks dimpled, brows lifted. "We'll find out. You're sure you won't try to kill him if he kisses me?"

Ethan turned the thought over in his mind. Tried to picture it—Nico kissing Peter—and busied himself with his lunch. The idea frightened him. Thrilled him. Made him eager for it. When Peter hummed, prompting an answer, Ethan tipped his head. "We'll have to see, won't we?"

Peter laughed in his throat. He linked his ankle around Ethan's boot and swayed their tangled feet. "You're the love of my life, Ethan Shaw," he whispered, poking at a carrot at the bottom of his bowl. "That'll never change."

Ethan's heart lurched. *You perfect idiot,* he thought and met Peter's dulce-brown eyes. "And you're mine, Peter Vásquez. Even when you bring home dead seals."

"Handsome seals," Peter corrected.

Ethan laughed, snorting like a schoolboy.

Chapter Eight

After wandering the market and spending a thoughtful hour on the beach, Ethan arrived at the lighthouse. Three shadows cross the domed windows on either side of the front door. His belly was full, his spirit lighter, but anxiety still spiked at the sight of people—presumably not Nico—prowling around his home. He buried his nose in his scarf and sighed, breathing in the scent of laundry soap and day-old cologne. The shadows scurried. When the door cracked open, Nico peeked outside.

"You have guests," Nico said and flicked his gaze toward the living quarters. "Clients? I don't know. People are here."

"And you let them in?"

The selkie shrugged. "What else was I supposed to do?"

"*Not* let them in," he seethed and walked inside.

The first thing Ethan noticed was Nico Locke's attire. Instead of borrowed sweaters and loose pants, he was dressed in a fitted shirt and dark-washed denim. An unfamiliar leather coat hung from the rack, and a utility pack slouched against the wall next to discarded shoes piled by the door. The second thing Ethan noticed, after he'd forcibly glanced away from Nico, was Lucia Belle leaning against the kitchen island and a woman pacing like a caged tiger.

"Good afternoon." Ethan hung his coat and uncoiled his scarf. "I wasn't expecting company."

"Mary Whitt needs a spell." Lucia, swathed in a sweaterdress and knee-length gardening boots, arched a sharply penciled eyebrow.

"I do; I need a spell," Mary snapped. Her thin mouth folded into a frown. Lines fissured outward from the corners of her lips. She had crow's feet, a wrinkled forehead, and a mop of ash-blonde hair.

Ethan had seen her at the market before, slinging faux flowers and knock-off lily oil—argan mixed with perfume—to foolish tourists. He'd also seen her at the docks, batting her eyelashes at sailors and fishermen during the swampy summer months.

"You're the witch, aren't you?" Mary continued. "You're the one who can make things happen?"

"I can't *make* anything happen, Miss Whitt. But I might be able to assist you if you tell me what you need." Ethan brushed past Nico and stepped over Lucia's crossed boots. He filled the kettle at the sink.

Mary stopped in her tracks and folded her arms. "My ex cheated on me with a busboy from the pub."

"And?"

"And I want you to make her pay for it."

Ethan laughed. A single, raspy *hah*. "That's not a service I offer."

"Then what do you offer?" Lucia asked, interjecting with an impatient sigh.

"I'll pay you." Mary gritted each word through clenched teeth. "That bitch deserves—"

"To be at peace." Ethan spoke over her. "I won't harm your ex, but I will try to mend your heart if you're open to it."

The lighthouse quieted. Lucia hummed, smiling wryly. Mary considered the offer. Her eyes trailed the window. When Nico took two, three, then four mugs out of the cupboard, Ethan wrinkled his nose and said, "I didn't offer."

Nico narrowed his eyes. His auburn hair was slicked away from his bold, bony face. "And here I am thinking you're generous."

"I'll take some tea," Lucia purred and turned toward Mary, nodding. "I'd consider his offer, honey. Angry hearts take a while to heal. Time you don't got."

Ethan poured steaming water into the cups Nico had set on the island and gestured to the tea cabinet. "Help yourselves, I guess." He added a chai bag to his cup and met Mary's guarded eyes. "Five hundred for the spell."

"Excuse me?" Mary laughed, loud and brash. "You're kidding, right? For what, exactly? To *mend* my heart? Make the hurt stop?" She croaked, voice waterlogged. "That's rich coming from a man like you. Witch bitch with no—"

"Two hundred for one night's sleep," Ethan barked, snapping his teeth at her. "I'm sure it's been a minute, right? Since you've slept peacefully? I'm sure you've been lying awake, wondering what a busboy had that you didn't." He watched her wilt and snarl like a possum. "Call me a bitch in my own home again, and I'll give you warts. Understood?"

Magic afflicted the lighthouse. Turned the air inside out and made everything slow and heavy. Lucia sipped their tea. Nico did the same, leaning on the counter with his eyebrows raised and a mug perched against his mouth.

Mary trembled. Her fingers formed fists, knuckles whitening. She nodded tightly, though, just as Ethan thought she would, and reached into her beaded purse. She slapped folded bills into his palm. "If I don't sleep, I'll come back for that."

"If you come back, I'll turn you into a walrus," he teased, voice slippery and mocking. Still, he pocketed the cash and kicked a chair away from the table. "Sit."

Mary plopped into the chair, clutching her purse to her stomach. "Will it hurt?"

"At first, yes." Ethan attempted to focus his thoughts. To stop staring at the place near the refrigerator where he'd kissed Nico. To stop following Nico's slow breath, to stop searching for his shadow on the floor, and his reflection on the window. He wanted to be done with this, but he didn't think he'd be rid of Mary Whitt without sending her home with some sort of spell.

He took a wine glass from the cabinet and plucked a rosemary stem from the bushel above the sink. Rubbing his thumb and pointer finger over a blackened wick, he coaxed a flame to appear atop a pillar candle. "Her name?"

Mary gulped. "Cressida."

"How long have you loved her?"

"Four years."

"How long has it been since you lost her?"

The woman sucked in a tiny, fragmented breath. "Three days."

Ethan silently called for magic, asked for assistance, for an audience, and held the rosemary over the flame. Slowly, it ignited. Magic swirled between his ears, crowded his throat, turned his stomach. He placed the smoldering herb on the table and caged it with the wine glass, trapping smoky plumes.

"Look at me, Mary," Ethan said.

Mary lifted her face. She was a solemn woman, lined by time but pretty in her plainness. She carried years on her slouched shoulders and cleverness in her eyes. Pain too. A terribly sad anger.

"Nico, open the window, please," Ethan said, angling his chin over his shoulder.

The latch unfastened, and the window slid open.

Ethan turned over the glass, brimming with smoky tendrils, and held it out to her. "Think of her and drink."

She blinked, confused. "Drink...?"

"Yes, drink," he said again. "Now, if you'd please."

Mary brought the glass to her lips and tilted it, sucking in the smoke. Her eyes welled, and her body shook, and she choked on a stifled sob. Once the smoke was gone, Ethan took her jaw in a firm grip and positioned his fingers like a pinched claw before her lips. Nico made an uncertain noise, but Lucia said nothing, just sipped their tea and waited.

Magic was a fickle thing. Ethan felt it like a quick-footed hare, jostling about inside her, collecting heartbreak and rotten love. Not everything, not all of it. But enough to let her rest until morning. He reached past her teeth and found a tendril of magic wriggling near the roof of her mouth. *Come here. Let me be rid of you.* He pinched the writhing smoke and yanked, causing Mary to cough and sputter. Finally, the love loosened. Ethan pulled it from her like a smoke-wire and shooed it out the window. The smoke darted about in panicky jolts and finally escaped.

"Shut the window," he said, sighing.

Nico closed and latched the window. He cleared his throat, face a little paler, pupils a little wider. "Is it...is it done?"

Mary breathed heavily. She splayed one hand across her heaving chest, feeling over her blouse. "Thank you," she said, surprised. Her throat flexed around a slow swallow. "And this'll last until—"

"Morning, probably. Lucia can make you an herbal blend for the rest, I'm sure." Ethan leveled Lucia with an irritated glance. *You will*, he said with his eyes. *Don't you dare bring her back here.*

Lucia Belle tipped their chin in a polite nod. "Hard part is done. C'mon, Miss Whitt."

Mary stared at Ethan. She was one of a handful in Casper who'd made their way to his lighthouse and asked for a spell. Most people were too superstitious. Too afraid of the necromancer who'd played God. But when comfort ran dry with family and sermons stopped ringing true at church, people always found a witch.

"Only one night?" Mary asked, hardly above a whisper.

Ethan added a spoonful of honey to his tea. "That's all you purchased," he said, eyeing her with an icy glare. "Have a good night, Mary." As she slipped her shoes on at the door, he cleared his throat. "And, Lucia." They turned, granting him a lazy once-over. "Even friends inquire about proper invitations, correct?"

They snorted and laughed under their breath. "Sure, sweetheart." They pursed their lips in a quick air-kiss. "Good evening, gentlemen."

The front door opened and closed. Footsteps crunched the gravel, fading.

Nico slurped his tea. "So, that was batshit."

"Bringing you back from the dead was batshit. What you just saw is a typical Friday." Ethan drank from his mug, swallowing honeyed mouthfuls despite the heat. "You got your things from the inn, then?"

"Yeah, I did. Paid my tab too."

"Good."

"Do you and Peter have plans for dinner?"

"Not that I'm aware of."

Nico ran his lip across the edge of the mug, still leaning against the counter, looking comfortable and familiar in the small kitchen. "We could go out?"

"Or order in," Ethan proposed.

"Or order in," he echoed. He toed nervously at the grout between tiles and kept his nose tipped toward his tea.

Ah, yes, here it is. The awkward knowing. The unspoken certainty. Nico had kissed Ethan that morning, and Ethan had kissed him back, but the selkie wasn't aware that Peter had given any sort of blessing. Had encouraged it, even. Watching Nico's tense expression morph from pensive to worried caused a laugh to bubble in Ethan's throat.

"*What?*" Nico barked.

"Easy, darling. Everything's fine," Ethan said. *Darling.* He'd never used the term for anyone except Peter and Miranda's half-feral housecat. "We can go out if you'd like, but there's not much to choose from in town. The storm warning might shutter a few places early, but we've got the pub, the café, Darika's food truck..." He paused, glancing at the ceiling, thinking. "Oh, a deli, and Antonucci's."

"Antonucci's is an Italian place, isn't it?"

Ethan nodded. "Bread baskets, Alfredo sauce, tiramisu. They've got it all."

"I have—" Nico patted his front pocket. "—my wallet back, so I can repay you and Peter for your hospitality—"

"You don't have to do that—"

"I want to." Nico finished his tea and glanced at the door, jutting his chin. "Peter's home."

Sure enough, heavy steps grew closer, and the door creaked open.

Peter sighed. Shrugged off his dewy coat, swiped away his beanie, and said, "Evenin'. Qué tal?"

Nico shifted his eyes to Ethan, a question lingering in his creased brow. Ethan didn't speak Spanish, but he'd joined the Vásquez family, so he knew enough to get by.

"We're fine," Ethan said, answering for them both. "How was the rest of your day?"

"Long." Peter scrubbed his hand over his beard, smoothing the short, coarse hair on his cheeks and jaw. His eyes hovered on Nico. "Did you get things settled at the inn?"

Nico nodded. "I did. Are you feeling up to going out? Ethan mentioned an Italian restaurant."

"Sure." A smile twitched on Peter's mouth. "Let's check your bandages first though. How've you been feeling? Better?"

"Still itchy but better." Nico pushed away from the counter and sat in the same seat Mary had occupied minutes ago. "Doesn't hurt as bad anymore."

Ethan retrieved the last of the salve from the fridge. "Let's see, then."

Nico worked his long-sleeved shirt over his head. His gaze was flighty, flicking between Peter and Ethan. He swallowed hard, and his fair skin reddened. "What is it?"

Ethan openly stared at Nico's lengthy torso and broad chest and rosebud nipples. Peter did too.

Carefully, Peter stepped around the back of the chair and touched the fae markings on Nico's collarbone. "You're easy to look at," he said. "That's all."

Ethan brought the salve to the table. "Relax," he murmured and undid the clip holding his bandages in place. "And stop acting surprised."

"I *am* surprised," Nico whispered through clenched teeth. His brows pulled together nervously, and he worried his lip with his teeth.

Ethan hummed and traced the dent where Nico's sternum bent inward between his pectorals. "Be still, fae-beast."

Nico froze. His breath came in soft, trembling puffs as Peter curled his palms over spotted shoulders, and Ethan went to work cleaning his wound. The gash had shrunk to a small, red seam.

"You heal quickly," Ethan said and framed the cut with dainty fingers. He knelt at Nico's side, dragging his gaze from the split flesh to his face. "If I stitch this now, you'd be able to swim as soon as tomorrow."

"Do it," Nico said, blushing like a damsel, still as a viper.

Ethan nodded curtly, but he couldn't avoid the splinter in his heart. *He's really going to leave.* He forced a smile. "Peter, get my kit."

Antonucci's Ristorante was always busy on the weekends, but the eatery was particularly crowded that night. Ethan sat between Nico and Peter at a square table draped in a white cloth, sipping cherry wine from a stemless glass. Nico and Peter faced each other on opposite sides of the table, silently scanning their laminated menus. Silverware clanked on fancy dishware, hushed chatter filled the room, and tealight candles flickered inside repurposed mason jars, casting a gilded glow across each tabletop.

Before they'd left the lighthouse, Ethan had sewn together Nico's busted skin, pushed a needle through healthy flesh, and pulled, resulting in a clean, pinkened line caged by thin thread. He'd flinched, of course, as most people would, but he hadn't hissed or whimpered. He'd just studied Ethan's face and stayed still with Peter's thumbs poised at the notch where his shoulders met his throat.

Ethan wished he could see the future. Find out where the night might lead. Nowhere, somewhere. He took another sip. Wine soaked his tongue.

"What're you two having?" Ethan asked.

"Risotto, I think," Peter said, tapping his menu.

"The fish," Nico said, predictably. "You?"

Ethan hummed. "Ribollita."

A server brought them a basket of warm bread. After they'd placed their orders, Peter poured oil and inky vinegar onto a plate for dipping, and the trio ate quietly, exchanging nervous glances the same way teenagers on a first date would.

Finally, Peter asked about Nico's family, his life back home, what it was like to travel alone, and Nico told stories of his mother and his aunt and his sister, women with sharp teeth and sharper minds, and spoke at length about sunning on glaciers, escaping pods of hungry orcas, hunting elk on land and penguins at sea.

"It gets lonely," he admitted, nodding his thanks as Ethan poured him more wine. "Most of the people I grew up with have paired off and started families."

"Why haven't you?" Ethan asked.

Nico shrugged, holding fast to the silence while their food was delivered to the table. "People like us marry young. I wasn't ready to commit to a life with someone, and now..." He forked his fish into pieces. "I had opportunities—good ones with good people—but I think I've missed my chance."

Ethan furrowed his brow. "How old are you? Twenty-six? Twenty-seven?"

"Thirty-three," Nico said, laughing softly. "I'm an old man where I'm from. Most breeding pairs have two or three pups by now. Like I said, I had the option, just made different choices."

"Sounds like you might've broken some hearts too," Peter said.

Nico popped his lips and finished the rest of his wine. "A few."

"Do you still want a family?" Ethan asked.

At that, a hush fell over the table. Nico glanced from Ethan to Peter, and Peter glanced from Nico to Ethan, and neither of them attempted to speak. Starting a family was an off-limits topic. Child rearing was a nonstarter. Ethan appreciated their concern for his bruised heart, yet something like sandpaper still scraped his insides.

"I'm not a baby bird. We can talk about children without me falling into hysterics, can't we?" Ethan asked, resisting the urge to snap.

"Sorry—yeah, I do," Nico blurted, face flushed. "I don't know if I'd make a good parent, but I'd like to try."

"And there's no one you fancy?" Peter asked, shooting a cautious glance at Ethan. He spooned rice into his mouth. "From your colony, I mean."

"No one I haven't already screwed things up with," Nico said and forced a pained smile. "And as much as I love my homeland, I think I'd prefer to stay outside the colony. My family's wonderful, but fae culture is a bit insular, to put it plainly."

"Understandable," Peter said.

The conversation dwindled. Ethan ate slowly, spooning hot soup into his mouth and trying desperately not to think about his own shortcomings. Peter and Nico had been right to try to dodge the subject of children, but he would absolutely *not* be letting them know that. *Save the selkie, Ethan*, he chastised himself. *It'll make you feel whole again.* He stared into his bowl, fighting against the sting in his nostrils.

"You've seen the northern lights, haven't you?" Nico asked, peeking at Ethan and Peter through his lashes.

Peter shook his head. Ethan did too.

"Even being this close? What a shame." Nico tsked.

"Casper is remote," Peter said, shrugging. "We've seen flickers of them from parts of the island, but we're too far from Greenland or Iceland to enjoy the whole show."

"It's beautiful. Like watercolors, almost. But brighter, more vibrant. They move." He lifted his hand, waving his fingers above the table. "Dance high above the horizon and catch on the water. Ice holds the color, you know. Acts like a mirror." Nico's mouth curved, tenderness like an aura radiating around his face. "I could take you." He nodded thoughtfully. "I'd like to take you."

Ethan's heart reached between his ribs. "I'd like to go."

Peter nodded. His smile twitched, eyes softening in the low light. "Me too."

They cleaned their plates, and Peter argued with Nico over the bill. In the end, Nico aggressively stomped to the host station to make sure the bill was charged to his card, and Peter insisted on covering the tip—*at least, Nico. C'mon, be reasonable.*

Once the squabble was handled, the three wandered toward the rocky beach, minding their feet as they took the stone staircase to the sand. From there, beneath the high, black cliffs, Ethan gazed at his lighthouse—*their* lighthouse—as the crescent moon skipped across rippling waves. Smoke billowed from skinny chimneys peppering the skyline, and the ocean sang a familiar song.

Ethan watched Peter trail Nico through the darkness. He stood at the edge of the tide as his husband kissed the selkie they'd saved, on that beach, on a cold, clear Friday evening. Nico Locke leaned into him. Their noses brushed, and their breath fogged the air. *Ethan*, he saw Nico say, lips stretched, tongue touching the back of his teeth. How strange to feel his heart rupture and rebel and restart. How comforting to brace for jealousy and find hope instead.

Ethan faced the moon again. He breathed because breathing seemed sensible; he wanted to remind himself it was possible to breathe right then, to inhale and exhale in the midst of change.

A hand—Peter's hand—found his palm, and lips—Nico's lips—brushed his temple.

"You haven't baked in a while," Peter said, following Ethan's gaze to the white sickle cut across the blackness.

Nico stood beside him, chin tipped downward, watching Ethan watch the moon.

"I could make a Skúffukaka," Ethan said.

"What's that?" Nico asked.

"Cake," Peter and Ethan said in unison.

Nico stifled a laugh. "Cake," he parroted, nodding. "I like cake."

Ethan smiled at the sky and stepped backward, making for the staircase. It'd been a long time since he'd made something sweet. Peter and Nico followed him, boots smashing sand then stone, dirt then gravel. After unlocking the front door, shoes were unlaced and kicked away. Coats hung on the rack with flannel scarves.

We could all use something sweet.

"Heat the oven," Ethan said and rolled up his sleeves.

Chapter Nine

The kitchen became a mess of spices, bowls, flour, whisks, and sugar. Ethan tore open a bag of dark chocolate with his teeth and tempered the chips. Nico leaned over his shoulder, gazing at the melted treat, and hummed pleasantly. His hand was a timid weight on Ethan's tailbone. Standing in front of the island, Peter plucked jars and vials up one by one, inspecting the faded labels.

"Babe, which one of these is vanilla?" Peter asked, adjusting his glasses.

Ethan poured the warmed chocolate into a bowl with oil and coffee. "Use the Tahitian vanilla. The label is a bit faded, but it should be next to the wax paper. Don't forget baking powder too."

Peter made a pleased noise. "Oh, this." The scrape of a whisk came and went and then the clank of the mortar and pestle. "Anise, right?"

Ethan sucked chocolate from his pinky finger and nodded. He stepped away from the stove and combined the mixing bowls, wet ingredients with dry ingredients, before picking up the pestle. The many-pointed spice gave way, crumbling into a fine powder with every twist of Ethan's wrist. He dumped the anise into the batter, gave it a quick whisk, then tipped the bowl over an oiled baking tin.

"Won't take long," Ethan said and slid the tin into the oven. "Twenty minutes, maybe."

Nico took three mugs off the drying rack next to the sink and pointed to the half-filled coffee maker. "Anybody else?"

Peter's face lit. "Sure, thanks."

Ethan almost said yes, but he remembered Nico's fertility recommendations—*stay off caffeine*—and shook his head. He couldn't revolve his life around possibility, chance, lost time. Couldn't keep himself trapped in the same toxic mental cycle. *Maybe this month, maybe next month, maybe a year from now. If I lift my legs higher, if I stay on my back, if I eat healthier.* But this *maybe*, this *if* seemed insignificant compared to the rest. Something he could try without heartache, like eating the snow plum.

And perhaps a part of him would always try. He knew the bottlenecked fear he'd carried for years had driven him into a spiral, but how does a witch rework a ritual he'd never paid attention to? How does someone snap a heartbreaking habit in half?

Breathe. Peter is right there. Inhale. *The sea couldn't keep him.* Exhale.

In the pit of him, buried under magic and memories, Ethan Shaw knew the answer. *Let it go.* But letting go of Katia, of something that'd been disastrously out of his control, took bravery he never gave himself permission to muster.

Breathe.

"I'll have some tea, actually," Ethan said. He filled the kettle and turned on the stove.

While the cake baked, scenting the lighthouse with cocoa and almond, Ethan steeped his peppermint tea, leaned his forearms on the island, and listened to Peter and Nico talk about the ocean, and religion, and magic. He chimed in here and there, sipping, laughing, smiling.

Nico narrowed his eyes and grinned as Peter breached the space between them and looped his finger around the gold chain above the selkie's collar. The crucifix was small and plain and left a dent on Peter's thumb.

"And what would your God think of me, huh?" Peter asked. The crucifix dropped to Nico's chest. "The fisherman who cast the net that caught you?"

"The *captain* who cast the net that caught me," Nico corrected. The timbre of his voice vibrated Ethan's skeleton. Peter blushed furiously. "I'm not sure, to be honest. Can't say I know the mind of God."

"And me?" Ethan asked, scorching his bottom lip on the edge of his mug. "You may not know the mind of God, but I'm sure he'd have something to say about a witch."

"Who's to say witchcraft isn't godhood," Nico dared. He met Ethan's gaze and tilted his head, cheeks brilliantly red, eyes blue as a glacier. "Thou shalt not worship false idols, and yet—" He clanked his coffee mug against Ethan's cup. "—here we are."

Everything beneath Ethan's navel tightened. *Worship.* He swallowed hard. As if Ethan Shaw might be something holy, as if his magic could possess the same rites and mysticism as the Bible itself. His body flushed at the thought. The look in Nico's half-curtained eyes and his sly smile spoke volumes. He knew what he'd done to Ethan. What he'd undone too.

The oven beeped—*thank Hecate*—and Ethan slipped his hands into mittens to retrieve the dessert. Both Peter and Nico crowded around him like hogs, sniffing the air, making small, raspy noises as he carefully set the hot tin on the stove. Ethan batted them both away and poured vanilla syrup over the top of the cake.

"You've outdone yourself, darling," Peter murmured, chin resting on the slope of Ethan's shoulder.

Ethan smiled. "Well, we haven't tasted—*hey!*" Laughter tumbled off his lips.

Nico slid a rather large bread knife through the cake, cutting a hefty square from the corner. "No need to ogle it when we can eat it."

He didn't bother with a fork, just dug his fingers into the slice and brought sticky cake to his mouth. He repeated the motion and held a piece out to Peter, who minded Nico's digits, daintily nipping at the dessert, then Ethan, who tried to keep his composure as he suckled at Nico's fingertips, swiping crumbs away with his tongue.

"It's rich," Peter purred. He broke a piece off of Nico's slice and popped it into his mouth. "Really rich."

"Richer than normal," Ethan said. He furrowed his brow and grabbed a fork, catching crumbs with his hand as he took a bite. It was made with dark chocolate, so heaviness was expected. But the vanilla should've gentled the flavor.

He kept eating. Licked syrup from his fork and sighed, perturbed. "Hmmm... I mean, I didn't change the recipe. Peter, you..." He glanced at the kitchen island where spices and oils were laid out and capped. "You used the vanilla, right? You..."

His grip slackened. *Oh, no.* The fork clattered on the tile. *Fucking hell.* Ethan made a wounded, embarrassing noise, and stared at the sallow droplets at the bottom of the siren marrow vial.

The nearly *empty* vial.

"Yes, I used the vanilla. Almost all of it," Peter said. He crouched and collected the fallen silverware. "You okay?"

"I like it," Nico said, nodding. "Doesn't taste too rich to me."

Ethan's lips hovered apart. He stared at the vial, heart hammering, breath shortening. Closed his eyes. Reopened them. *Shit.* His lungs shriveled. It felt like lightning in his veins, like a sparkler had ignited in his stomach.

"Ethan, you're pale," Peter said, suddenly serious.

"I..." *Speak.* Ethan squeaked instead. "I..."

"What's wrong?" Nico asked, one cheek bulged with cake.

Well, it was too late for dishonesty. They'd eaten the cake; they'd ingested the marrow. He held the vial between his thumb and pointer finger.

"This is siren marrow," Ethan said, matter-of-factly.

Nico choked on the cake. He gulped coffee and winced, shooting Ethan a look of disbelief. His pupils dilated, his cheeks flared, and he laughed cruelly. "You're kidding," he barked, flicking his eyes from the vial to Ethan. "Jesus fucking Christ, Ethan."

"Says the Catholic seal." Peter chewed his cake. He tilted his head curiously, shifting his gaze between Ethan and Nico. "What've I missed? What's happening?"

"Your husband drugged us," Nico said.

Peter's eyes widened.

"Technically, he drugged us," Ethan exclaimed, jabbing his finger at Peter.

"*What...?*" Peter wrinkled his nose.

Ethan gripped the counter behind him and stared at the floor, trying desperately to level his breathing. "Look, I went to the herbiary to get ingredients for the salve"—he gestured wildly to Nico—"and the shopkeeper had overheard gossip about our issues at the apothecary"—he gestured wildly to Peter—"and offered to give me a good deal on an aphrodisiacal stimulant called siren marrow. So, I bought some from Lucia—"

"The Lucia who was just here? With that rude-ass woman who bought a spell from you?" Nico asked.

Ethan let his eyes slip shut. "*Yes.*"

"Wait, a spell?" Peter interjected. "What spell?"

"A run-of-the-mill heartbreak spell," Ethan hissed, flapping his hands. "Listen! I bought the siren marrow for *us*," he said, glaring at Peter. "But then we talked, and everything was fine, so I put it away for another time, like, like our anniversary or...fuck, I don't know, something! But now you've dosed the cake, and we've eaten the cake, so..." He let his hands fall dramatically, smacking his sides. "Here we are."

Nico took a large step backward. "Have either of you ever—"

"No," Ethan snapped.

Peter shook his head. His expression wobbled between shocked and terrified. "I've smoked weed a few times."

Nico yelped out a helpless laugh. "Awesome. Great. Perfect."

"This isn't the end of the world," Ethan assured. "We'll be fine."

Nico raised his eyebrows and rolled his lips together, staring through the window behind the sink. He flexed his hands. Breathed with a sharpness Ethan was suddenly, viscerally attuned to. Ethan wet his throat and gripped the counter harder, enduring a surge of woozy euphoria. It came on strong, dizzying and fiery.

"Okay..." Ethan sucked in a trembling breath. "Okay, so... so, maybe..."

Peter cleared his throat, took Ethan by the wrist, and tugged him toward the bedroom. "Let's talk."

Ethan gave Nico a panicked glance and stumbled along, halting inside the bedroom as Peter shut the door.

"Okay, one, I don't know what's going on," Peter blurted, whispering. "Two, I feel weird—maybe not *weird*—but... Yeah, no, weird. Anyway, what..." He trailed his knuckles along Ethan's cheek. "What's next? Where do we go from here?"

"I don't know," Ethan said, and it was the truth. His pulse quickened as if he'd been rewired with an insatiable hunger. He felt too hot. Too tight. Too open. His mouth watered, and his cunt clenched, and it became difficult to think, rationalize, focus.

Lucia Belle's voice fluttered through his cloudy mind. *You'll be irresistible to each other.*

"We do this together or not at all," Peter said and glanced at the door. "This isn't what I expected but..."

"He's here. We're all here," Ethan said, nodding.

Peter sighed. "Are you okay with this?"

"Yes," he said, and thought of Nico, and thought of Peter, and thought nervously of the intimate, immediate future. "Are you?"

Peter's pupils stretched toward the edges of his irises. "Yeah," he said and dragged his hand from Ethan's jaw to his throat. "Together, right?"

"Together," Ethan assured and touched the back of Peter's hand, tracing his knobby knuckles. He opened the bedroom door.

Nico Locke paced in the living quarters, taking long strides from the kitchen to the coatrack. He wrung his hands and chewed his lip, moving like a fretting beast. He halted and turned toward them, shoulders held tightly, gaze owlish and too fast. He looked caught. On edge. Keyed up and ready to strike.

"I can go," Nico said. He leaned toward Ethan and Peter with his feet firmly planted, flaring his nostrils. "I should probably go." He whirled toward the door. "I'm going—"

"Go if you'd like." Ethan extended his hand and steadied his voice. "Or come to bed with us."

Ethan held his breath. They'd landed in an impossible situation. Fallen into one another after such a short time, after a taste of *could be*, and there was nothing left to shy from. No reason not to give in.

"Please," Ethan added, hardly a whisper, and fought against the urge to close his eyes when Peter's lips graced his neck.

Nico halted and met Ethan's gaze, waiting for another confirmation, for assurance, for *something*. When Ethan gave a curt nod, Nico crossed the room in a single breath, framed Ethan's jaw in his palm, and kissed him firmly on the mouth. *Oh.* Ethan's head spun. He whimpered. *Oh, my.* Locked his knees and reached backward to grip Peter's buzzed head, forcing him to bite harder, to suck at his throat. Trapped between those two men, Ethan Shaw felt powerful.

Ethan kissed and was kissed. Opened his mouth for Nico's hot breath and warm tongue, broke away to latch onto the column of his throat, to place a mark there and listen to Peter kiss Nico, Nico kiss Peter. A thumb—Peter's thumb—toyed with the button on Ethan's jeans, and a hand—Nico's hand—snaked over his hip, behind him, groping for Peter's waist.

"We need rules," Nico said, startlingly abrupt.

Ethan stumbled backward into the bedroom. "What kind?"

"You're *married*," he said, exasperated. "C'mon."

"You know we've been trying to start a family," Peter said. He detached from Ethan for long enough to peel his shirt away, revealing his toned, brown chest flecked with wiry hair, and his tapered middle. "Let's not do anything to compromise that."

Ethan narrowed his eyes, but the confusion waned. He met Nico's heated stare and gave a curt nod. "Feel free to touch me, just..." *Please, touch me.* "Be mindful of..."

"Of where I come?" Nico asked.

Heat raced into Ethan's cheeks. "Exactly."

Nico cast his gaze around their bedroom, catching on the messy dresser, the unmade bed, and the antique clothes cabinet. He startled when Ethan gripped the bottom of his shirt, eyes flashing.

"Is this okay?" Ethan asked.

Nico nodded. His shirt came away easily. "How far are you willing to go?"

Ethan looked over his shoulder at his infuriatingly beautiful husband. "As far as you're willing to take me," he braved, hyperaware of his own clothes, his own skin, his own body—imperfect and rebuilt. Adapted. Insecurity needled his throat. "I might not be what you're expecting," he said, sneaking another shy glance at Nico.

Peter reached beneath Ethan's sweater and pushed the garment up, over his binder, higher, to his chin, and away. "You're beautiful, mi querido."

The siren marrow turned each touch into an invitation. Peter kissed his shoulder, and Ethan's knees wobbled. Nico feathered his fingers along the pouty skin above his hip bones, and his breath came short. It wasn't until Peter had helped him out of his binder that he understood the gravity of their situation. The primal intent. Not until Ethan grasped Nico's hand and brought it to his small breast—asking him to squeeze, to explore—did the last shred of hesitation fall away. It was then that Nico kissed him again, when Peter unbuttoned his pants, when Ethan was somehow stripped to his socks and pressed into the bed. He hadn't expected to find Peter's wanting lips, to be kissed with a fever by his husband while Nico spread his legs, nipped his thighs, and opened his mouth over his cunt. The sensation was unimaginable. Unlike anything he'd felt before—intimacy but far more intense—as if someone had uncorked every place in his body where pleasure could possibly be stored.

Peter pushed his hand through Nico's hair, holding him in place, and inhaled what Ethan exhaled. Ethan's chest stuttered, nipples pink and peaked. He moaned, welcoming the confident push of Nico's fingers inside him, probing his cunt, gathering wetness, and then slipping lower. Nico teased his rim before he buried one, then two fingers inside Ethan's ass, stretching him on bony knuckles. Ethan expected pain and found none. His body simply opened; muscles nurtured by the marrow.

He came with Nico's mouth around his swollen clit, his fingers buried to the hilt, and Peter's teeth on his nipple. Ethan bucked off the bed, yelping like an animal, enduring a wave of white-hot pleasure that spread outward from his core. He couldn't grasp time after that. He was touching and being touched. Helping Peter and Nico out of their clothes and trying to keep up with kiss after kiss, movement after movement, touch after touch.

Peter's cock disappeared between Nico's lips, and Ethan felt the marrow sink into his bones, into his mind, and blur the lines between sensual and grotesque. He followed Peter's guidance—*on your knees, yeah, like that*—as Peter pulled Nico to his feet and un-capped a bottle of lube he'd fished out of the nightstand. Ethan knelt before Nico. The selkie's lashes fluttered when Peter worked him open and filled him on an eager thrust. Ethan took Nico into his mouth. Kept his eyes trained on the pleasure crossing Nico's face. Felt his cock harden and twitch at the back of his throat and loved the weight of him on his tongue, adored how Peter reached around and cupped his skull, gripped hard, forcing him to take Nico deeper, to gag and choke and loosen his jaw.

They fucked like people without reservations. Nico whimpered, gasping raggedly while the sound of their bodies meeting rang through the bedroom. He came in hot ropes, slicking Ethan's gums and throat. Semen dirtied his lips and coated his chin on a sticky cough. Ethan's empty cunt throbbed. *Ached.* In all his life, he'd never felt as rabid as he did right then. As starved and willing.

The marrow ate away at his insecurity. Made it easy to moan and demand, to do things he'd never done. Strange, to push the taste of Nico into Peter's mouth on a feverish kiss. To stumble to the bed, land on his hands and knees, and find his hips seized, his back hole slathered with lube and filled on a clumsy thrust. Strange, to be fucked by Nico, ravaged by him, knowing Peter was watching. Even stranger to clutch his bedsheets and beg—*harder, faster, more*—until he was lifted, grappling for purchase on his husband's shoulders. Peter kissed him and breached his cunt. The reality of having two people, being filled completely, overwhelmed him. Especially that night, sex-drunk and thrumming with untapped want, chasing high after high, orgasm after orgasm.

No fantasy could compare.

Ethan dug his fingernails into Peter's biceps and rested the back of his head on Nico's shoulder, suspended between them, small and malleable and worshipped. Their raspy voices and quivering breath disrupted the quiet, and Ethan paid mind to the place Nico grabbed him, how his webbed hands fit around the underside of his thighs. Peter's jaw slackened. His expression tensed whenever Ethan spasmed around his cock.

Heat climbed into his abdomen and roiled like the sea. It knotted at the base of his spine, cinching tighter, *tighter* until Ethan's body jolted, and he cried out. Peter moaned against his neck, holding him by the waist, and snapped his hips faster, harder. Nico went rigid, lips pressed to Ethan's nape, and spilled inside him, holding him still until Peter tripped into his climax on a held breath. Ethan was so, *so* full, swollen with it, with them. His cunt flooded, surged, slickened. His lax body squeezed and leaked.

They stayed awake well into the night. At one point, Ethan was on his back, gazing dreamily at the ceiling while Peter fucked him. Right after, he was flipped onto his stomach and taken by Nico. And sometime near midnight, he was riding his husband, voice pitchy and uncaring, movements fast and messy, as Nico slipped his tongue into Peter's mouth. They milked pleasure from one another. Toppled around the bed and coupled on the floor. Kissed and breathed and beckoned one another. Near sunrise, Peter massaged Nico's prostate, one arm curled around his middle, holding him above Ethan, fingering him until he spurted across Ethan's stomach, and as day broke across the horizon, Ethan kissed them in long, slow passes, moving from one mouth to the other while the effects of the siren marrow began to dwindle.

The bathroom wasn't big enough for three people, but they crowded together in the steamy shower anyway. Their feet bumped in the tub. Peter looped his arm around Ethan's waist to keep him steady, and they didn't speak, didn't ask *are you okay*, didn't bother with reassurances. Peter kissed the underside of Nico's jaw, and Ethan chased rivulets in the hollow of Peter's clavicles. They soaped generously. Stood under the scalding water until the heater ran cold. Toweled off and dragged themselves back to the bedroom. They stripped the bed and replaced the ruined sheets with quilts and blankets from the linen closet, then tangled close in the thinning darkness.

Ethan didn't remember falling asleep. He listened to Peter breathe, counted the steady flow of Nico exhaling on his nape, and closed his eyes, lulled by the ocean, held by his husband, tucked against the handsome selkie he'd caught and saved and wanted to keep.

CHAPTER TEN

I t was late in the day, the bridge between afternoon and evening, when Ethan cracked his eyes open. Sunlight glowed on the backside of the curtains, shadows stretched across the bedroom floor, and Nico and Peter slept soundly beside him. He swallowed to wet his achy throat and shifted onto his side, ignoring the soreness blooming in his pelvis. Peter's chest was pressed to Ethan's spine, one arm thrown carelessly over his waist, and Nico faced him, lips serenely parted.

Ethan followed the fine lines around Nico's eyes, the faint scar on his cheek, and thumbed at his strong jaw. *Thirty-three. I see it now.* He thought he'd feel different after last night, after what they'd done, after who he'd turned into. Ethan thought he would've been embarrassed or ashamed. Instead, he felt renewed. Midnight echoed on his skin. Left him satiated and pleasantly exhausted. Hungry too. He tapped Nico's nose and watched his lashes flutter, his throat flex, his breathing shallow.

Ethan's mouth made the shape of the word—*hi*—and Nico nuzzled closer, leaning into his palm. Nico laid his hand over Ethan's wrist, and Ethan mapped his face with smooth, tender touches, feathering his fingers over the bow of Nico's top lip, his high cheek, the line between his coarse brows.

They stayed like that, trading gentleness in a quiet room, foreheads pressed together, legs tangled under the old, musty quilt. Ethan hadn't expected Nico to be careful with him. He hadn't anticipated the slow drag of his webbed hand along the slight curve at his waist or his mouth to caress his freckled temple with such ease. But the deadly, daring beast that'd raged inside their garden shed was gone, and Nico Locke was lovingly tame.

Peter stirred, curling inward to breathe against Ethan's nape. "Coffee," he rasped and snaked his palm over Ethan's sternum, squeezing him.

Nico hummed in agreement and moved his hand from Ethan's wrist to Peter's forearm. "I can make it."

"Ignore him—stay here," Ethan said, earning a huff from his husband.

Just a little longer. Ethan framed Nico's ear with his hand and tipped his head against the pillow, granting Peter access to his neck. Stubble scraped his skin followed by Peter's chilly nose and soft lips.

"How'd those stitches hold?" Peter asked.

Nico grunted. "Fine, I think." He leaned back and lifted his arm, glancing at the black line drawn across his side. The blanket pooled at his waist. Mouth-shaped bruises peppered his hip bones, some indented with pale, crescent toothmarks, others blotchy and purplish. He glanced sideways at Ethan. "How're you doin'?"

Ethan snorted. "I'd like a bath, a massage, and pancakes, thank you very much."

"I'm sure we can arrange that," Peter purred.

"I'll get the coffee started." Nico slid out of bed.

Ethan watched him step into the jeans puddled on the floor and tug them to his hips, leaving the denim unbuttoned as he trudged to the kitchen. Peter ghosted his fingertips along Ethan's breast-bone, and they shared the sound of someone bustling around their kitchen. Ethan remembered last night in great detail. The drunken bliss of being strung between two bodies. Wanting to be devoured, captured, consumed. He remembered the intensity too. The inti-macy. He turned until their noses bumped and tipped his head, melting into a long kiss.

"Are you okay?" Ethan asked.

Peter pecked the side of his mouth. "Yeah, I am. Last night was..."

"A lot?"

"A lot."

"You enjoyed it though?" Ethan asked hopefully.

"I did." Peter's eyes shone like polished wood. "You care for him, don't you?"

"I..." Ethan paused, considering. "It's peculiar. I *enjoy* him. He hasn't left yet, and I'm already heartbroken, but it's different, I guess. I haven't been at the beginning of something in, oh, a decade. Longer, even."

"Thirteen years," Peter said and aligned his palm against Ethan's. He brought their hands above them, catching the last sip of daylight that shot past the curtains. His lengthy fingers engulfed Ethan's smaller digits. "*Like* feels juvenile after last night, but I do *like* him. I want to spend more time with him. Get to know him better."

"Me too," Ethan whispered.

There they were, Ethan Shaw and Peter Vásquez, holding on to each other.

"Coffee's done," Nico called. Mugs clanked on the countertop.

Ethan brought Peter's hand to his mouth, kissed his knuckles, and then crawled out of bed. He shuffled into a pair of clean sweatpants and didn't bother with his binder, just pushed his arms through one of Peter's flannels as he left the room.

Nico had also put the kettle on—*bless him*—and was sliding a log into the hearth. When the selkie turned, his eyes scanned Ethan's stomach, left exposed by Peter's unbuttoned shirt, and he smiled softly.

A moment later, Peter shuffled in, scratching his head, dressed in nothing but a pair of navy joggers and mismatched socks. "So, what the hell are we doin' with that?" He jabbed his finger at the marrow-cake on the countertop.

Ethan shrugged, lifting his eyebrows. "Siren marrow's hard to come by."

Peter wiped a smudge off of his glasses and put them on. "And we've baked it into a cake. It's not like we can extract it, darling."

"We'll freeze it." Ethan fastened the middle button on his shirt and fished a rectangular storage pan out of a cabinet beneath the kitchen island. "It'll last for six months at least. Probably a year."

"Which means you're planning on using it again?" Nico gestured between Ethan and Peter. "Last night was the third time in my life—my *whole* life—I've dosed on marrow, and you're stashing away a year's worth? Hardcore, seriously."

"Well, there's no good reason to waste it, is there?" Ethan hissed. Heat rushed into his face. He snarled through a mean grin. "And you didn't seem upset about *dosing* last night, so mind your manners. We'll save it for special occasions."

"Special occasions," Nico deadpanned. Sarcasm soaked each word.

Ethan clipped a lid atop the glass container. "Now that we know how potent it is, we can take it in smaller amounts. We're all adults, aren't we? No harm in having it on hand."

"Don't use it too much," Nico warned. He smiled sheepishly. "Might screw with your libido."

"Noted," Peter said.

Once the cake was placed safely in the freezer, Ethan fixed himself a cup of tea and brought it with him to the washroom. It didn't take long for Peter to plod after him, shooing him away.

"I got it," Peter said. He ran the bath, added rose oil and Epsom salt, and kissed the top of Ethan's head. "We'll make breakfast when you're done."

"Dinner," Ethan corrected, wrinkling his nose. "Or... Yes, I guess it's breakfast, isn't it?"

"Breakfast for supper." Peter snorted a laugh and pinched Ethan's chin before he slipped away, leaving the door cracked.

Steam curled away from the water. Ethan took a long, cleansing breath, stripped off his pajamas, and sank into the tub. Thankfully, Peter had learned a thing or two over the course of their marriage and left the harsh overhead light turned off, allowing Ethan the opportunity to savor a bit of well-earned darkness. He tipped his head against the porcelain and closed his eyes, paying mind to the ache in his core, radiating low in his back and deep in his hips. Remnants of last night bruised him, inside and out, and served as a reminder that he wasn't nineteen anymore. Marathon sex wasn't something he could bounce back from with an energy drink and half-assed yoga.

He set his knuckles in the groove where his thighs met his pelvis and massaged the flexor in each hip, working soreness away, then stretched toward the ceiling. Dragging a powder-blue razor over his skin, he sheared fair hair from his legs.

Last night, he'd brought a long-lost version of himself back from the dead. He'd unburied the Ethan Shaw that'd panicked on the docks three years ago, summoned an unknown spell to save his husband, and said *yes, let's try* afterward.

The truth bubbled upward, something he'd known and never admitted. Fear—that awful, relentless fear—had stolen his ability to speak, to ask, to be open. Hurricane Katia, her raging seas, and all her power had snatched away his autonomy. He'd given it freely—that sense of self, that youth, that freedom—in a botched trade for Peter Vásquez. *Maybe it was never a child.* He opened his eyes. Light ribboned the door. Maybe the cost had always been *this.*

The horror. The hope. The mourning.

Ethan dipped beneath the water and surfaced, tasting rose and salt, newness and release.

You have him, he reminded himself and listened to Peter's rough laugh—*there*—accompanied by Nico's lovely voice—*yes, there*—and etched security into his heart. *You have him, you have him, you have him.*

Ethan had lost him, yes. But he'd hauled Peter back to this plane, to this lighthouse, to their life. And he could breathe again. Could settle again. Could live again.

Breathe, Ethan. He inhaled shakily. *Breathe.* Exhaled.

Ethan had brought Peter back, and he'd brought Nico back, and he'd brought himself back.

Once his hands and feet were pruned and the soreness had waned, Ethan uncapped the drain and toweled off. He dressed again and swiped his hand across the fogged mirror, revealing his reflection. He pushed his hair out of his face and craned to assess the bruise at the base of his neck. Hickeys at twenty-nine. How delightfully depraved.

Ethan left the washroom damp and flowery.

"Where's your syrup?" Nico asked.

He pointed to the pantry. "Next to the canned caramel, I believe. Pancakes, then?"

Nico and Peter made pleased noises.

The night had hardly begun, but the candelabra scattered gold around the lighthouse. Jarred candles in the windowsill sparked with a snap of Ethan's finger while shadows reigned over Casper. In the distance, the ocean sent waves crashing against the cliffside, bending sacred lilies and slapping seaweed onto the shore. Nearer, Ethan sucked batter from the side of Nico's hand and smiled against Peter's mouth while an oddly shaped pancake sizzled on the cast-iron griddle. Their home rang with stories and laughter. Butter, honey, and cranberry jam perfumed the kitchen. Wood crackled in the hearth, and the kettle whistled.

At one point, Peter rested his nose against the top of Ethan's head and said, "You smell good." At another, Nico jutted his chin at Peter and narrowed his eyes, licking syrup from his mouth in a quick swoop. They touched tenderly, reverently. Bumped into one another near the sink, pressed sticky kisses to cheeks and lips and shoulders, fed one another with fingers and forks.

It was brilliant and easy, their togetherness. Peaceful and right.

But Nico's phone still buzzed, and he still answered. "Aine, hi," he said and shot Ethan an apologetic smile as he crossed the room. "Yeah, I'm shipping my things... Tomorrow, probably..." He closed the front door behind him, but Ethan could still make out each word. *Yes, Auntie, I'll be careful*—in his low, rough growl—*Oh, c'mon, I'm all stitched up and fine to swim.*

"I didn't think it'd be this soon," Peter murmured, his arms a soothing weight around Ethan's waist.

Ethan sighed. "I did."

Peter clucked his tongue. "Don't do that, c'mon."

"Don't do what? I'm not *doing* anything."

"We'll invite him back for Yule." Peter set his chin on Ethan's shoulder, swaying back and forth. "You can seduce him with your clementine cookies, and I'll cook up a few grouse. We'll take him to the festival downtown, make him try reindeer kabobs. He'll come; you'll see."

Ethan wasn't sure his heart could handle more hollow hope. He nodded, though, if only to please his husband, and ducked away when the door opened.

"Sorry," Nico said, glancing between Ethan and Peter. "My aunt was checking in."

"No worries," Peter said.

Ethan stood at the sink, facing the window. He busied himself with the greasy griddle and their dirty utensils. Soaped, rinsed, soaped again, rinsed again. Nico stayed quiet for a drawn, tense moment, but the silence broke around Peter's big sigh. Chatter started again, first about their breakfast-for-dinner, then about Casper, and soon enough, the three men were situated around the hearth, draped in blankets atop the cot. Ethan sat between Peter's thighs and stretched his legs over Nico's lap, listening to the fire crackle. It was this he'd miss. This new beginning.

Nico ghosted his hand along Ethan's dainty foot, smoothing his palm under the cuff of his sweatpants. "I don't know how to thank you," he said, so quietly Ethan almost didn't hear him.

You could stay, Ethan thought, but that wouldn't be fair. "You don't have to," he said instead and tried to smile.

"You saved my life." Nico's strong bone structure didn't match the softness on his face. He relaxed his brow and folded his mouth into a tiny frown, more open and honest than he'd been since he awoke in their shed. "I haven't been a very *friendly* guest—"

"I would argue that," Peter muttered. Playfulness warmed like liquor.

Nico gave a sheepish smile, and a blush fanned his nose. "I'm not good at this," he said and squeezed Ethan's ankle. "I'm not good at companionship, or niceties, or..."

"If you're trying to tell us you have no manners, we've certainly noticed," Ethan said, snorting.

Peter shushed him.

"I'm trying to tell you that I'm not sure what happens next," Nico admitted. All the fae-born confidence he typically carried fell away, and he gazed at them with wide, questioning eyes. "But I don't want this to end here because I'm afraid if it does, I'll be a memory for you, and you'll be a curse for me." He swallowed hard, searching the floor, the hearth, Ethan. "I'll have no peace. I'll think about you constantly, so I'd like to see this through."

"Yet you're leaving tomorrow." Ethan let his eyes slip shut, ashamed of the venom in his voice. "I'm sorry; I didn't mean that."

Nico's lips thinned and his brows pulled together. "If I could come back—"

"Of course, you can," Peter said. His chest rumbled against Ethan's spine. "Yule is next month. There's a festival, good food, merriment all 'round. Come back to Casper and share it with us."

"Ethan?" Nico set his thumb against the arch of his foot. "Are you okay with that?"

"When you first arrived, I told you you'd be landlocked for at least a week. It's hardly been a few days, and you're ready to swim to Reykjavík." Ethan knew how childish he sounded, the way he bit through a whine as if undue anger might chase off the heartsickness.

I don't want you to go. He hated himself for being selfish. Hated his neediness. *I want to keep you.*

"But sure, fine, I'm okay with that," Ethan said. "Come back for Christmas, and don't skewer yourself on a reef this time—no, *no*, don't you dare—" He tried not to smile and failed miserably, suddenly caged against Peter by Nico's strong arms bracketing his waist. The selkie loomed over him, brushing his nose along Ethan's cheek.

"You're a mean little witch," Nico whispered.

"And you're an ungrateful beast," Ethan said, but it was hardly the truth. He felt Peter heave another sigh, and held his breath when Nico closed the space between them, kissing him firmly on the mouth. Ethan spoke against his lips. "You'll text us when you get to the city, right?"

Nico smiled crookedly. "Yeah, I can do that."

"You will." Peter seized Nico by his square jaw and tugged him into a kiss. "I won't have you lost in another fisherman's net."

"Heaven forbid." Laughter bubbled up and out of Nico, the good, rough kind that shook his shoulders.

Ethan laughed, too, as did Peter, and all around them things changed, evolved, stayed the same. The evening lengthened toward midnight, and candles dripped wax onto the table, and the sea shushed beyond the tower. Ethan Shaw was there with Peter Vásquez, and they were holding on to Nico Locke.

M orning arrived too early.

Ethan woke to a seagull's shrill cry while the navy sky began to brighten. Reality tipped into clear view, sharpening dull, dreamy fragments into a picturesque moment—Nico Locke, asleep on his back in the middle of their bed, breathing evenly. His gorgeous, spotted collarbones and slack, spattered face. Auburn hair more burnt than normal, shining brick-red in the blue hour. Beside him, Peter slept with his face aimed at the window, his dark scruff a stark contrast to the white pillow beneath his cheek. Ethan's chest constricted. They were both so, *so* beautiful.

It wasn't long before Nico opened his eyes, and not long after that, Peter stirred awake. They didn't speak, didn't rise or slip from the bed. Instead, Ethan crowded against Nico and fit their lips together. Kissed him until his mouth opened, and his breath stuttered, and he moaned softly between their coupled lips. Kept him there, prying hungrily at his mouth. Peter suckled at Nico's throat, bit and nipped and worried his fair flesh. Ethan kept him in their bed, gasping and whimpering. Edged him, cruelly and lovingly, massaging the head of his cock while Peter stroked his shaft, and didn't stop, didn't let him come until he said their names, until he whined and his lashes fluttered, until Ethan was sure he wouldn't forget Casper, and the lighthouse, and the men who lived there.

They stayed in the bedroom for an hour. Ethan came with Nico's fingers jammed inside him, working him through a slow, heated orgasm, and Peter groaned when he emptied into Nico's mouth. But after that, their bodies limp and sated, the bedroom became a humid, used-up space, too full and too lived-in to keep them.

Nico cleaned his teeth before he left. He drank a cup of coffee, slung the bag containing his precious pelt over his shoulder, and stood in the doorway, dressed in leather and denim, letting a chilly breeze coast through the lighthouse.

Ethan thought it brash to hold on to anger, to pout in the face of discomfort, so he approached Nico tenderly and traced the gold crucifix strung around his neck. "Christmas, then."

Nico nodded. "Christmas it is."

"We'll ship your things to the city." Ethan kissed him chastely at first, then pulled away and brought the crucifix to his mouth, setting gold between his teeth. "Be safe, Nico Locke."

Nico hummed, a growlish sound. He kissed Ethan again, longer this time, deeper, steadier. Kissed Peter, too, leaning into him on one foot as boat horns blared in the harbor. He didn't say *goodbye*. Didn't bother with *see you later*. Nothing. The selkie simply met their eyes, Peter first, Ethan second, and took the gravel road toward the beach. His footsteps echoed on the slick rock, and his tall, lean frame shrank in the distance, disappearing altogether after three, four, five heartbeats.

Peter said, "We'll see him again," and rested his hand on Ethan's tailbone.

Ethan nodded but stayed quiet.

Goodbyes were difficult, so the trio had made a deal. In one hour, Peter would collect Nico's bag from the beach and take it to the post office. But in the meantime, while they waited for the tide to cooperate, Peter fixed a pot of coffee, and Ethan made tea. Fresh wood popped in the hearth, and life went backward. Eased into *before*. Peter sat in the recliner with a book in his lap, glasses perched on his nose, and a coffee mug balanced on the armrest, and Ethan watched through the kitchen window, hoping to glimpse a familiar pelt. *Spots shaped like skipping stones.*

It wasn't long before Ethan Shaw felt the lonesome pull inside him. The place where magic called out to itself in another. Wasn't long before he took the snow plum from the fridge, and a knife from the cutlery block, and followed that strange, ethereal tug to the garden and then the cliffside.

"What're you doin' out here? It's freezing," Peter said, stomping after him through the damp grass around their garden boxes.

But Ethan knew that tight, coiling ribbon in his core. Knew it was tethered to the magic—the life—he'd placed in someone else. He halted at the edge of the cliff and glanced downward at the lilies climbing sheer black rock.

"Look," Ethan said. He slid the knife into the snow plum and brought it to his mouth, gesturing at the ocean with the sticky blade.

Past the shoreline and the shelf, the riptide and the choppy waves, a leopard seal bobbed in the water, peering at the lighthouse.

There you are. I see you. Ethan turned toward his husband and cut another slice from the snow plum. Carefully, Peter bit into the fruit, sliding his lips around Ethan's fingertips.

"Te amo," Peter whispered, clutching Ethan's wrist. He kissed every knuckle, every line on his palm.

"I love you too," Ethan said, and when he looked toward the horizon, following magic and hope and Nico, the leopard seal was gone.

Not the magic though. Ethan smiled and tasted snow plum on Peter's lips. *Not the magic.*

Epilogue

Christmas Eve

"What'd you do?" Ethan whined, tearing open the decorative paper surrounding a squishy gift. He pulled a fine-knit, mustard-yellow scarf to his face, nuzzling the soft material. "It's gorgeous, Peter. Where'd you get this?"

"It's cashmere. My mother sent me a picture and asked if you'd like it. She shipped it a couple weeks ago." Peter took the scarf and looped it around Ethan's neck. "She loved your fudge, by the way. Everybody did."

Ethan clucked his tongue. "Well, if Paola Vásquez loved my fudge, then I know I've done something right." He flashed a grin and tilted his head, pecking Peter on the lips. "We'll Facetime with everyone tomorrow, yeah?"

"Of course. Your mother is meeting us at the festival?"

"She'll be there," Ethan said.

Snow fell past the window and dusted Casper's slanted rooftops and cobblestone streets. Farmers had moved their livestock into barns and heated stables, and winter crops were kept alive by greenhouse shelters. Chimneys billowed smoke. Local families and curious tourists wandered downtown, watching vendors ready their booths for the Yuletide festival the following evening. Specter Café offered their seasonal treats—leaf bread, ginger biscuits, vínarterta, and fruit cake—and a Christmas tree strung with white bulbs, faux candles, fresh lilies, and glittery globes stood proudly in front of the pub.

It was Christmas Eve, the time when people crowded around dinner tables, exchanged early gifts, and celebrated the rebirth of the year, and Ethan and Peter had filled the lighthouse with joy. A small potted evergreen sat prettily behind the hearth in front of the domed window beside the door, sparkling with multicolored lights. Garland was strung around the sills and doorframes, and wide-mouthed bells were clipped above each window.

Ethan handed Peter a neatly wrapped box. "Careful, now. It's not *exactly* fragile, but—" He mock-cringed. "—it's breakable."

Peter lifted his brows, adjusted his glasses, and peeled away the silver paper. "Qué va! You got me one?" He opened the box, revealing an electronic tablet.

"I already loaded ten books onto the account," Ethan said, quite proud of himself.

"Thank you, darling. I love it," Peter rasped and kissed him.

It was Christmas Eve, the time when people who'd been gone for too long arrived for the holidays. When miracles happened, and love grew, and nights lasted. Ethan glanced at the wrapped gifts beneath their tree and resisted the urge to splay his hand over his stomach.

Give it time.

It was too early to talk about the timid flutter in his stomach, like a moth beating its wings behind his navel. Too soon to take a test, too soon to visit the clinic, too soon to *know*. But Ethan felt it. That magical little life stirring inside him. He ran his palm between his hips, as if to coax another hop, another tiny spike in his core. *Yes.* Like wings, like hope. *There you are.*

"Where'd you go?" Peter cupped Ethan's cheek, guiding him into another kiss.

"Nowhere," he assured. He should've checked the casserole. Should've crawled into Peter's lap and whispered to him about the child—*their child*—growing inside him.

But the kettle whistled, and three heavy knocks sounded at the front door.

Peter smiled softly, laughing under his breath. "Told you he'd be early," he said, hushed.

Ethan pushed his forehead with two fingers. Excitement sparked, flaring hot in his chest. He crossed the room and opened the door, suddenly out of breath, suddenly laughing like a fool.

Muted light poured over muscular shoulders, illuminating a lean shape standing on their welcome mat. Snow dusted Nico Locke's weatherworn jacket, and his backpack hung heavy on his shoulder. He had one hand tucked inside his jacket, and his smile was as handsome and crooked as ever, mischievous eyes glinting under the porch light.

"Merry Christmas," Nico said and carefully removed a tiny, flat-faced creature wrapped in a too-big bow from inside his jacket. The kitten meowed as it batted the air. He shrugged, holding the snow-white creature out to Ethan. "Every witch needs a cat."

Surprise unspooled inside Ethan, accompanied by a short gasp. He laughed again, sharp and brittle, and scooped the kitten between his hands, cooing delightedly.

"You've outdone yourself, seal," Peter called from inside. "Coffee or tea?"

"Coffee, please." Nico lifted Ethan's chin and kissed him, walking him backward into the lighthouse. "Now you've got something of your own," he whispered. He dropped his pack by the coatrack, toed off his snowy boots, and scratched the kitten's head.

Ethan hiccupped through another laugh. He held the mewling kitten with one hand and laid the other over his belly. *Here we are. Alive and breathing, loved and safe. Here I am.* Held and holding life.

Holding life.

ALSO BY FREYDÍS ☽

Exodus 20:3

With A Vengeance

The Gideon Testaments

Heart, Haunt, Havoc

Wolf, Willow, Witch

Saint, Sorrow, Sinner

Acknowledgements

I'm extraordinarily grateful for the opportunity to bring a book about fertility, love, mental health, and polyamory to readers everywhere. To my editorial team, thank you for believing in this strange little story. To my friends, early readers, and inspirational peers, I value the time we spend chatting, brainstorming, and sharing space together—your talent and grace inspire me.

ABOUT ☽

Freydís Moon (they/él/ella) is a bestselling, award-winning author, tarot reader, and Pushcart Prize nominee. When they aren't writing or divining, Freydís is usually trying their hand at a recommended recipe, practicing a new language, or browsing their local bookstore. You can find their poetry, short stories, and fiction in many places, including *Strange Horizons*, *The Deadlands*, and elsewhere.

https://freydismoon.carrd.co

For information about the cover illustrator, please find **M.E. Morgan** here: https://morlevart.com/